THE TOLL ROAD BETWEEN THE STARS

Perseus Gate – Episode 5

BY M. D. COOPER

M. D. COOPER

SPECIAL THANKS
Just in Time (JIT) & Beta Reads

David Wilson
Jim Dean
Lisa L. Richman
Scott Reid
Katrina Able
Timothy Van Oosterwyk Bruyn

Copyright © 2017 M. D. Cooper

Cover Art by Andrew Dobell
Editing by Tee Ayer

Aeon 14 & M. D. Cooper are registered trademarks of Michael Cooper
All rights reserved

PERSEUS GATE: SEASON 1 – THE TOLL ROAD BETWEEN THE STARS

TABLE OF CONTENTS

FOREWORD 5
LAST TIME ON PERSEUS GATE 7
SABRINA'S CREW 8
MAPS 9
CHANGE OF FATE..11
FAREWELLS 16
PERRY STRAIT 19
BOARDED 29
ELLIS REACH...37
THE PERRY 47
CHEEKY'S OUTING 58
SLOP & DINNER 70
THE BOMB 96
PERINA...98
THE DEAL WITH DERRICK..107
BETTER THAN YOU FOUND IT...114
JUMP GATE 120
ON THE ROAD AGAIN 134
THE BOOKS OF AEON 14...139
ABOUT THE AUTHOR 143

FOREWORD

Before you dive in, I'll warn you that this one's a bit shorter than the previous novellas in the Perseus Gate series. I had the story outlined and knew what it was about, but it just refused to get any longer than about 100 pages.

I could have forced it, added some additional subplot, lumped in backstory about some new person that the crew meets on their journey, but I felt as though that would have taken away from the main thrust of the story, which is very much about Jessica coming to grips with a few personal issues.

The other reason why this one's a bit shorter is because of the grand finale; *The Final Stroll on Perseus's Arm* will be much longer than the previous books—at least another 50-70 additional pages worth—and I want to get to that story so that I can wrap it up, and finally catch Perseus Gate up to the events of Orion Rising.

This story also serves another purpose: to examine how all space is not as empty as what we see around our star.

Sol is in a relatively nice neighborhood. Our fellow stars we travel with keep at a reasonable distance, not disturbing our Oort cloud, not going supernova (thank the stars), and generally leaving our dear Sol alone.

But in other regions of the galaxy, in stellar nurseries, and globular clusters, stars are very, very close to one another. So close, in fact, that there could be as many as half a dozen within the volume of our Sol System.

Those conditions are not ideal for humans in any form. Be it trying to terraform worlds while that many stars are glaring down from above (and bathing you in radiation), or even just trying to navigate with all the flotsam and jetsam, plasma, coronal mass ejections, and everything else going on.

Most nebulae are like this. Superheated gasses, plasma, stars being born, and stars dying are everywhere. These are not the homes of sedate stars like our Sol; the type of star that will live relatively peaceful lives for ten-billion years or so.

Such places often birth stars that only live for as little as a few million years. Massive A-spectrum blue giants that consume fuel at an alarming rate before exploding in supernovae that create the heavier elements required for stellar systems like ours to form.

But you don't want to live there, and if you do, there are a lot of places you don't want to go. Even without FTL—and the fear of running into mass in the dark layer—very often, you simply can't get to there from here.

And that is where Jessica and the crew of *Sabrina* find themselves, flying through a narrow channel in the Stillwater Nebula, inhospitable space on either side, and a route that will take them through a less than savory locale.

M. D. Cooper
Danvers, 2017

LAST TIME ON PERSEUS GATE

In The Last Bastion of Star City, the crew of *Sabrina* came to Star City, a massive dyson sphere built around a neutron star.

There, Jessica, Trevor, and Iris went into *The Dream*—the matrix-like artificial world where lifetimes are accelerated to move humans closer to ascension at a rapid rate.

There, Jessica, Trevor, and Iris created sixteen AI children who became Bastions, the defenders of Star City. Those children successfully protected the city from the Orion Guard and will now protect The Dreamers—the final few billions of humans who have not yet ascended and remain in The Dream.

Now, the crew of *Sabrina* must tear themselves away from Star City and continue their journey to New Canaan, facing the long, perilous path through the Stillwater Nebula.

SABRINA'S CREW

Cargo – Ship's Captain
Cheeky – Pilot
Erin – AI embedded in Nance
Finaeus – Passenger
Jessica – First Mate
Hank – AI embedded in Cargo
Iris – AI embedded in Jessica
Misha – Trader picked up in Naga System
Nance – Bio/Engineer
Piya – AI embedded in Cheeky
Sabrina – Ship's AI
Terry – Mechanic recruited on Gallas
Trevor – Supercargo and muscle

NOTE: When *Sabrina* is italicized, it refers to the ship, but if Sabrina is not italicized, it refers to the AI. Yes, this would be much simpler if the ship and AI did not share the same name, but you try telling that to Sabrina!

Just so you stay on her good side, never call the ship "**the** *Sabrina*"; it really gets on her last synthetic neuron.

PERSEUS GATE: SEASON 1 – THE TOLL ROAD BETWEEN THE STARS

MAPS

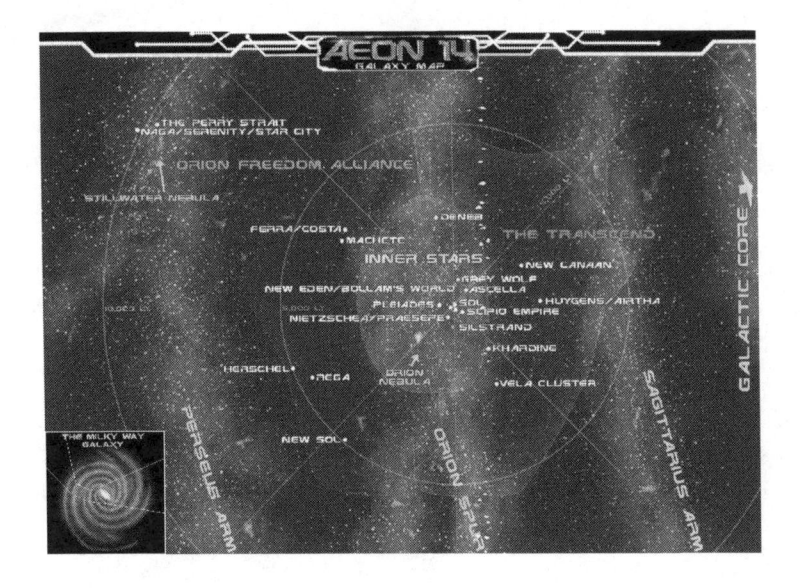

CHANGE OF FATE
STELLAR DATE: 11.24.8938 (Adjusted Years)
LOCATION: Manhattan, Star City
REGION: Star City System, Perseus Arm

Jessica stood next to the ship her children were giving Terry for her journey home. It felt surreal to Jessica that her own children were doling out starships.... She let out a long breath and placed her hand on the hull, wishing the craft a safe journey amidst the stars.

"You worried about my ship?" Terry asked as she approached, carrying a crate of fresh produce for the trip.

"It's been a while since it's been out in the black," Jessica said. "Just giving it some good vibes."

Terry set the crate down and approached Jessica, running her hand along the hull as well. "It's a good ship. I've checked her over, and so have Nance and Finaeus. She'll get me home."

"Are you sure you want to go?" Jessica asked. "We only just got started on our adventure."

"Seriously, Jessica," Terry said with a shake of her head. "Your 'just getting started' is most people's 'incredible adventure of a lifetime'."

"Sorry we scared you off, then," Jessica replied.

"That's not it, Jessica. I know I've had trouble putting it into words, but when it comes down to it, I think I felt like I was abandoning my people. The Serenity Primus is an oppressive feudal system—something I learned about during some studies in The Dream. Knowing that my friends and family will live and die under that system, never knowing anything else.... It's just not something I can let happen."

"I understand that." Jessica nodded. "I couldn't stay to fix it, but I couldn't bear the thought of you staying there forever...so I took you away."

Terry took a step forward and placed her hands on Jessica's shoulders. "And I thank you for that. You have no idea how much this has meant to me. I never had any clue of what is out here. I still barely grasp it, but I know I have to go back and make a change."

"What are you going to do?" Jessica asked.

"I don't exactly know yet." Terry gave a nonchalant shrug. "A revolution of some sort. Maybe it will be peaceful, maybe it won't. You never saw how much it sucks for people in the lower rungs. Who knows..." her voice trailed off for a moment, "at the very least I could lead an exodus to Star City. Tanis told me that they would welcome us. Either to settle in a biome, or to enter The Dream."

"Those are some lofty goals," Jessica said. "I wish you the best of luck. Who knows? We could see each other again as well. Some way, somehow, we're going to see my kids again."

Terry nodded. "Of course, you will. I imagine once you get to New Canaan you can get back by jump gate—I mean, it's how you got out to the Perseus Arm in the first place. Come to think of it, I'm not sure why Finaeus can't build a jump gate here right now."

"Stars...." Jessica sighed. "We've been round and round on this one. Finaeus has a whole host of reasons why it's a bad idea to build one here."

"Still seems shorter than a twenty-year flight," Terry said.

"*Seems* that way." Jessica nodded again. "But it would still take some years to manufacture the mirrors. Finaeus is also worried about initializing a jump gate so close to the nebula and all this dark matter. I guess once the wormhole-thing is established it can pass through anything, but initialization can be tricky. I guess they run the risk of sending you anywhere."

"I bet you're all a little leery of that," Terry said with a grin.

"Just a smidge."

"I can also imagine that if the Orion Guard folks saw that Star City had jump-gate tech, they might get antsy and renew their efforts to get here."

Jessica sighed. "There is that, yeah. Not keen on putting the kids in danger—well, more danger."

Terry took Jessica's hand and leaned in to give her a kiss on the cheek. "Still can't believe you're a mom...of sixteen. You are unlike anyone I ever expected to encounter...ever."

"I'm sorry that we'll never be able to find out if there's anything between us," Jessica said. "I don't know what it is, but I find myself drawn to you, Terry."

A look of frustration clouded Terry's face. "Oh, *now* you say it? You flirt with me back on Gallas, drag me across the stars, wait 'til I'm about to leave, and then you drop the we-could-have-had-something bomb?"

Jessica pursed her lips. "I know. It was a jerk move. It couldn't have happened anyway. Trevor's a one-woman kind of guy. For this to work for him, I have to be too. But you never know. Life is long, and I'll meet you again. I know it."

Terry leaned back in and kissed Jessica on the lips. Not a chaste kiss either. One full of longing and desire.

"Not going to wait for you, purple girl. But if you come back, and are available…"

Jessica grinned and stroked Terry's cheek. "If I knew you kissed like that, I might have tried to convince Trevor."

Terry turned and walked away, grabbing her case of produce. "Well, too bad, Jessica. You missed a golden opportunity."

"Seems like it," Jessica replied.

<You just can't help it, can you?> Iris asked.

<Can't help what?> Jessica grinned. <She's the one who kissed me. Twice.>

<You don't think Trevor would mind?>

Jessica watched Terry walk up the ramp to her ship's airlock. <No, not really, not a goodbye kiss with a woman I'll never see again after tonight. He's not so insecure that something like that would upset him. If he can handle me beating him one hundred and sevenieen times in a row at Snark, he can handle this.>

<Do you know what I take away from all this?> Iris asked.

<What?>

Iris chuckled. <You all play way too much Snark.>

FAREWELLS
STELLAR DATE: 11.24.8938 (Adjusted Years)
LOCATION: Manhattan, Star City
REGION: Star City System, Perseus Arm

The celebration that night was held in the physical world, not The Dream. The kids used holopresences to take part, commenting several times on how the lighting in the physical world seemed 'off'.

"You know," Jessica said to Tanis after her daughter mentioned it, "we're sitting atop a massive sphere with another sphere overhead. The light here is entirely artificial. It's all but guaranteed to feel wrong."

"I know, Mom," Tanis replied. "It's not that, though. It's something about the contrast between light and dark. It's more pronounced here."

Jessica looked around and compared the scene before her to memories of The Dream. It looked the same to her, but then again, she saw things differently than her children—in both The Dream and the physical world.

"I'll have to take your word for it."

"I suppose you will, Mom."

Jessica studied Tanis, memorizing her face, committing her small ticks and quirks to memory. The urge to stay at Star City was strong, but Jessica knew such a future would be hollow; it would be trying to live in the past while her children grew toward a future she could barely envision.

"Mom, your mods give you an eidetic memory. You won't forget what I look like."

"We organics are fragile," Jessica replied. "You never know when a mod might fail and we need to rely on good ole neurons and our chemical memories."

"Sounds so dangerous," Tanis said with a shake of her head. "To trust everything that you are to electrochemical impulses in living tissue. It's a miracle humanity has managed as well as it has."

"Very illogical for an AI," Jessica mock-scolded Tanis. "You know that *because* it has happened, it is probable that it indeed would have happened."

Tanis snorted. "Don't quote probability at me. And I should add, there's nothing artificial about me. My siblings and I are the natural evolution of life. You could join us, you know. We've found a way to overcome the issues that foiled Johan when he tried to convert other advanced humans to Bastions."

"What?" Jessica asked. "To become two beings? One still as I am, and another with you?"

"Yes," Tanis replied.

No stronger temptation had ever been laid before Jessica. She chewed at her lip as she imagined a future as an AI, living in The Dream, or as a Bastion, or however she chose, probably ascending as an eternal being at some point.

But she also knew that a version of her would remain behind. And that version would feel so very, very alone.

"No," she eventually replied. "We *will* be reunited at some point. And then…who knows. Only time will tell."

Jessica wished she could embrace her daughter, and contented herself with placing a hand within the projection of Tanis's.

"Yes, Mother. Only time will tell."

PERRY STRAIT
STELLAR DATE: 04.19.8940 (Adjusted Years)
LOCATION: *Sabrina*
REGION: Perry System, Stillwater Nebula, Perseus Arm

Two years later...

"You thinking about them?" Trevor asked as he placed his hands on Jessica's shoulders.

She turned from the scan console on the bridge and looked up at her husband. "Yeah, it's hard not to wonder what they're doing."

"Hopefully not much," Trevor replied. "Just tending to their crop of dreamers and not fighting hordes of Orion ships."

"By now they'll have their own drone fleets," Jessica said. "Or they'd better. I gave them the blueprints. They could produce a million a year given their infrastructure."

Trevor laughed as he reached down for Jessica's hand. "I almost—*almost*—pity the Orion fools."

Jessica took his hand and he pulled her up into a warm embrace. "I don't regret it for a moment. Those were some of the best years of my life. And we'll see them again. I know it. Once we get Finaeus to New Canaan, he and Earnest will work out a way to get a jump gate that can target while that close to the nebula and we'll have regular trade with Star City."

"I think that won't be too hard," Finaeus replied from the comm auxiliary station in the back. "At least getting there will be easy. Getting back...well, if we make a return gate at Serenity, then we can do return jumps from there."

Jessica flushed. She had forgotten that the entire crew, minus Nance, was on the bridge as they approached the Perry System. It had been so quiet, and she'd been lost in her memories.

"I remember, Finaeus. We discussed the issues surrounding a gate at Star City for some time."

"OK, just making sure; it *was* a while back."

Jessica nodded, her thoughts still focused on the gate and its potential ramifications. "But if we built a gate at Serenity—which has a whole host of other issues associated with it—won't it cause Orion to perk up and take notice? Star City can protect itself against Orion, Serenity cannot."

"Oh, well, yeah," Finaeus said. "But in that case I think we can put it *in* Serenity Primus."

"What?" Cheeky asked, turning in her seat to look at Finaeus. "I love you dear, but some days I think you've lost your marbles."

"Well, not *in* in the planet. Gas giants like Serenity Primus get pretty inhospitable pretty fast. Just below the cloud tops. I think I could use the planet's gravity to counteract the proximity of the nebula's dark matter."

"And if it doesn't work?" Misha asked, a worried look on his face.

Finaeus shrugged. "Well, either you end up in some new, distant location, or you fly straight into the planet."

Misha shook his head. "So you're saying it's a bit risky."

"I guess," Finaeus replied. "But so's life."

Misha muttered something about how life with Finaeus was infinitely more so, and Cheeky laughed.

The bridge grew quiet once more and eventually Jessica said, "It's the long trip in the dark for us."

"Not so dark around here," Cheeky said, gesturing at the display.

Jessica looked out and smiled at the beautiful view.

For two long years they had taken the winding path through the Stillwater Nebula, and were nearly at the far side. But they had come to a choke point. Here the path through the nebula narrowed down to a small passage. And at its center was a star.

When they had first entered the nebula, they had expected it to be empty, devoid of settlements and interstellar traffic. What they had found was quite the opposite.

It turned out that there were many populated star systems. Isolated locations where people had built small, simple civilizations, far from FTL routes and the interstellar society that thrummed beyond the nebula's glowing borders.

While most stars born in Stillwater were large, hot blue stars, spewing radiation and inhospitable light, some were smaller—G or K spectrum—giving off moderate light, while still possessing enough of a stellar wind to push back the clouds and create a shield around their planets. From what they had seen, some of those stars even possessed marginally habitable worlds.

While saying sub-light trade 'flourished' in the nebula would be a stretch, it did exist, centered along the few systems in the narrow FTL corridor *Sabrina* traversed.

Somehow—except for a few leaks over the years—few outsiders knew of the corridor, and those who did were not inclined to share in the bounty that trade with the nebula brought.

In fact, from what they had learned, people who spilled the beans about the path through the clouds often did not live long enough to enjoy whatever reward they received for sharing the information.

That secrecy had caused *Sabrina*'s crew some amount of trouble during their journey, but not much more than they were used to encountering.

The Perry System would be the hardest test yet. Known as The Perry Strait, it sat in the center of a quarter-light-year stretch where no FTL was possible. Two months in, two months out. Following the portage, there was just a final ten-light-year hop and they'd be out of the nebula and back in open space.

Ahead, the Perry star—a young, angry, blue-tinged thing—thrashed in space, frequently ejecting coronal mass and blasting its radiation-laden winds in all directions.

Around the star system, the nebula was thick, drawn in by the star's gravity, in turn then repulsed by its winds. Jessica often found herself watching the nebula's clouds as they roiled, forming beautiful swirls that took millennia to take shape and then dissipate.

From *Sabrina*'s current vantage point, it looked as though the star was fighting against a death grip that the clouds had on it. And though it appeared dire for the Perry star, it would eventually prevail. It would take at least another five million years, but the star would eventually die a spectacular death, detonating in a supernova. When that happened, the blast would push the nebula back for light years, clearing a wide, open space through the clouds.

Of course, by then they'd all be long dead and humanity—and maybe even the AIs—would be long gone.

Trevor gave a languid stretch. "I'd best recheck our tags. We have two holds worth of stuff bound for Perry. What's our first target, Viceroy Station, or Ellis Reach?"

"Based on their current positions, I think we should hit Ellis first," Cheeky said before turning to look over her shoulder at Cargo. "Captain?"

"I agree," Cargo said. "Ellis is just a couple days out; Viceroy is at least four."

Jessica nodded and sat back at her console. "Then I'd best get us our lane into Ellis, it's first up on the outskirts." She pulled the frequencies for Ellis off the closest broadcast beacon and sent in a standard docking request.

Trevor leant over and kissed her on the head and Jessica smiled as she watched his broad figure turn and leave the bridge.

<*I need to shake this melancholy,*> Jessica said privately to Iris.

<*Yes, you really do, it's making your brain all weird.*>

<Maybe something exciting will happen here to take my mind off...you know,> Jessica said as she prepared a message of docking intent, as the locals called it, for Ellis.

<Seriously? I can't believe you'd jinx us like that. 'Something exciting'? We're doomed.>

<You don't believe in luck, or fate, or jinxing,> Jessica replied.

<Ha! After all these years with you, I'm starting to.>

With twenty minutes of light-lag, it took a few hours of back-and-forth with the station to establish an inbound lane to Ellis Reach. Once she had it set, and Cheeky got *Sabrina*'s burns plotted out, Jessica begged off bridge duty and called it a night.

The next morning, she had just started her second cup of coffee when Sabrina interrupted her thoughts.

<Hey Jessica, Ellis Reach just sent a message back that some of our cargo will need to be inspected before we dock. We're to bring our station-relative delta-v to zero and hold at a distance of a hundred thousand klicks.>

<And so the shakedown begins,> Jessica replied with a heavy sigh. <Folks back at Harvey System did warn us about how they operate in Perry.>

<We don't **really** need to trade here. We can tell them to go pound sand and fly right through,> Sabrina replied. <I wonder what it's like to pound sand.>

<Unsatisfying,> Jessica replied.

<I guess the saying makes sense, then.>

Jessica rose and walked to the coffee pot, topping off her cup. <Still, we're traders, we trade. If we don't trade, it looks unusual. Plus, from what the folks at Harvey told us, even if we fly on through they'll demand a toll. It'd be best if we didn't have to fight our way through this system.>

<Do **you** want to adjust our course, or shall I?> Sabrina asked.

Jessica chuckled. <Thanks for humoring me. It's all you, you're a better pilot than I am.>

Sabrina sighed. <I don't think so, Jessica, but thanks for humoring **me**.>

<What do you mean?> Jessica asked.

<I've run the sims a thousand times since the Grey Wolf Star...I'm ashamed to say it, but I don't think I could have saved Cheeky.>

Jessica paused half way up the ladder to the command deck. She was surprised that Sabrina had run sims on that rescue; even more surprised that she hadn't successfully saved Cheeky in those sims.

"What do you mean?" she asked.

<Well, if I do **exactly** what you did, then yes, I catch Cheeky. But you didn't take the most logical, most efficacious course. If I operate without the knowledge of your actions, I can never manage to get her. There's something...something

about 'flying with your gut', as Cheeky puts it, that I just can't figure out.>

<It's how we 'feel' the ship when we fly,> Jessica replied as she resumed her climb. <Cheeky's lowered the inertial dampening on her pilot's seat—as you likely know. It's genius, really. If she hadn't done that, I doubt I could have pulled it off. I've probably spent a decade flying in the black back at Victoria—I mean no dark layer drifting, and no grav drives— but actual flying. It may not beat your time on the clock, Sabs, but it was visceral. I learned how to fly by instinct there.>

<Is this where you talk about feeling the thrum of the ship and all that?> Sabrina asked.

Jessica nodded absently as she walked onto the empty bridge. <Hey, wasn't Misha supposed to be on duty?>

<He's in the head,> Sabrina replied.

Jessica sat in the pilot's seat and watched as Sabrina altered their burn to lower their delta-*v* and move them into a parking lane. The burns were textbook, but they lacked finesse.

<Have you ever considered trying something that's suboptimal, and then overcompensating for it?> Jessica asked.

<I've realized plotted maneuvers were suboptimal and then corrected,> Sabrina replied. <Is that what you mean?>

Jessica shook her head. <No, it's not. I mean deliberately get too close to another ship, or dip too deep into an atmosphere and then have to burn hard to get out.>

<Jessica, that sounds dangerous.>

<Yeah, but you see Cheeky do it all the time, and she's an amazing pilot.>

Sabrina sighed. <That's because she has a gut. I, however, am gutless.>

Jessica laughed aloud. <Sabs, you have more guts than you give yourself credit for.>

<Thanks, Jessica. I'll think about what you suggested. Maybe I can learn to develop my gut.>

<I like where your head's at, Sabrina.>

BOARDED

STELLAR DATE: 04.20.8940 (Adjusted Years)
LOCATION: *Sabrina*
REGION: Perry System, Stillwater Nebula, Perseus Arm

"Nice little bird you have here," the tall, rail-thin woman said as she stepped through the airlock.

"I'm Captain Cargo. You must be Inspector Brooke," Cargo said as he offered his hand.

Brooke looked at it like it may as well have been a snake and didn't offer hers in response. "I am, and I'm here to make sure you're not hauling any contraband and that all the tariffs are paid."

"Let us know what we owe," Cargo said in even tones, "and we'll have no problem making payment. We've already secured a local system account and have registered a store of platinum as collateral."

Brooke nodded. "Yes, I see that you've registered that with Stillwater Stellar Bank. I'll check it over as well to ensure you have the amount you said you did, and let them know to pick it up when you dock."

"You work for the bank too?" Cargo asked.

Brooke winked and flipped a lock of her azure hair over her shoulder. "I take care of all sorts of odds and ends."

"That's good to hear. Sounds efficient," Cargo replied, not exactly happy to hear it, but it did make the whole extortion racket easy if he only had to deal with one person.

<Sounds like she's on the take with everyone,> Sabrina commented privately.

<Not as though it's anything new,> Cargo replied.

It was unusual, however, for a woman like Brooke to come onto a ship alone. Usually there was a troop of soldiers stomping around looking menacing and generally getting in the way. For some reason Brooke seemed to think she was perfectly safe boarding strange ships on her own.

Either she was very dangerous, brave, stupid, or the Perry System's reputation of ruthlessness was strong enough that Brooke believed no one would mess with her and risk retribution.

He found her confidence and bravado rather alluring.

<I see the way you're looking at her,> Hank said privately. <The woman's a snake.>

Cargo grunted. <I'm not looking for a life-partner here. You have no idea how hard it can be to serve on this ship with all these women under you, but you can't fraternize.>

<Did you mean to have all that double entendre in there, or are you just that repressed right now?> Hank asked.

Cargo didn't reply, and led Brooke to the holds containing the shipments bound for Ellis Reach and Viceroy Station.

When they reached Cargo Hold 3—where the platinum was stored—she cracked open the crates of ingots and rummaged through them, pulling out random samples and testing their quality.

"Looks like you're on the up and up here," she commented. "Given this stuff's quality, and the current exchange rates, you'll need to set aside three hundred and eleven kilograms for the bank. I'll let them know that you'll have it ready when you dock.

Cargo almost swore at the number, but drew a deep breath. "Are you certain? That seems…like a lot."

"Lot of platinum on the market lately; drives the value down," Brooke replied with a shrug as she scooped out a fistful of ingots. "Let's see now…this feels like about the right amount."

"For what?" Cargo asked.

Brooke laughed. "Seriously? You have to ask."

Cargo sighed. "No, I suppose not."

<Not even a pretense here,> Sabrina commented. <That's never a good sign.>

<Yeah, means there's probably no uncorrupt authority to appeal to,> Cargo replied. <We'll send Jessica in to figure out

the local power structure and the rules to play by. She's good at that.>

<Yeah, she sure fits in well with criminals for being a cop,> Hank added.

<You realize you're speaking on the shipnet,> Jessica chimed in.

Cargo didn't have a chance to say it was intentional before Brooke straightened and gave him a sharp nod.

"I just need to meet your crew to ensure that your roster matches and get DNA samples from each, and we'll be all set."

<Notice how the 'freight inspection' didn't actually involve inspecting any of our freight?> Hank commented.

Cargo frowned. "What do you mean 'get DNA samples'. Don't you have security arches that do that when we dock?"

"Yeah," Brooke nodded. "But you're not docked, and you don't get to dock till I clear you, so get your crew assembled in your main bay or wherever you hang out so that I can check them over."

<I'll pass it along,> Sabrina said.

Five minutes later Cargo led Brooke into the galley where the crew was sitting at the table, except Nance who was leaning up against the counter. Without a hazsuit on, to Cargo's surprise. Her DNA sample, however, was already collected in a trio of vials on the counter beside her.

The moment Brooke entered the galley her eyes locked onto Jessica. "You're…"

"Katarina," she offered her hand. "I'm the first mate here aboard the *Sacred Retribution*."

Brooke took a step closer, bending her willowy form over as she peered into Jessica's face. "You look familiar, have you ever passed through the Perry Strait before?"

"No," Jessica said with a laugh. "Not even close."

"Huh," Brooke said as she straightened. "Coulda sworn."

"I guess I have one of those faces," Jessica replied with a shrug.

"You?" Brooke laughed, a strange warbling sound. "No, you most certainly do *not* have one of those faces. You have the exact opposite of one of those faces."

"Uhh…OK."

Cargo watched as Brooke took DNA samples from the crew. They had no need to worry about what she collected, their nanotech would make sure that Brooke's scanner saw only what they wanted it to.

Brooke took her time with Jessica, taking three separate samples before announcing herself satisfied and turning to Misha.

Once Brooke was facing away, Jessica made a rather rude gesture at the inspector. The gesture turned into a series of full body motions that nearly had Cheeky laughing aloud while Cargo waved frantically for her to stop.

Done with Misha, Brooke spun about to take a sample from Trevor and Jessica was caught in a rather awkward position with one leg up on the table, and a banana in her mouth. Her recovery was less than smooth as she placed her other leg on the table and pretended to smoke the banana nonchalantly.

<Real mature, Jess,> Cargo commented privately.

<I'm trying to loosen up.>

<During an inspection in the one-step-above-pirates system?> Cargo shook his head.

<Sorry, I'll try to be more circumspect.>

Cargo snorted aloud and Brooke's sharp gaze darted to him. "Something on your mind, Captain?"

"Lots, actually," Cargo replied. "Like, what's the best food joint on Ellis Reach? I'm dying for a good burger and we've been out of meat for three weeks."

"You're a real funny crew," Brooke said, scowling at them all. She turned and approached Nance. "And you. I'm not using your sample; I have to take my own."

"No," Nance replied with a shake of her head as she stared down Brooke. "You're not taking your own sample. You'll use mine."

"Another comedian, great," Brook said as she reached out with her sample extractor.

Nance caught her wrist and shook her head again. "No, you'll use my sample. Pick it up."

Brooke stared into Nance's eyes for several long seconds before nodding. "Fine. I'll use your sample."

<Damn, Nance, you do the negotiating from now on,> Jessica said on the crew's private channel.

Nance's net avatar shrugged. <Just have to be firm with these types. She doesn't really want trouble, only acts tough so that she doesn't have to put up with shit.>

"OK, I'm all set here," Brooke said. "If you'll escort me to the airlock, Captain Cargo, I'll be on my way."

"Gladly," Cargo replied.

<You're going to ask her to meet you at a bar on the station, aren't you?> Hank asked.

<I am. Jessica and Cheeky are going to try to get me laid soon if I don't do it myself. Stars, our AHAP is starting to look good at this point.>

Hank laughed. <I can activate Addie if Brooke turns you down, get her primed with the right programming.>

<It was a joke, Hank, a joke.>

<You got it, Captain, I'm already spinning her up.>

<Hank!>

ELLIS REACH
STELLAR DATE: 04.20.8940 (Adjusted Years)
LOCATION: Ellis Reach
REGION: Perry System, Stillwater Nebula, Perseus Arm

Ellis Reach was a curious station. For starters, it had a local ordinance against referring to it as a 'station'. It had to be referenced properly as 'Ellis Reach', or just 'The Reach'.

From what Jessica had picked up on the local feeds during their approach, the denizens tended to call it 'The Reach', which was fine by her. Ellis was the name of a boyfriend she'd had back in Athabasca who had been a complete dickhead.

The Reach was a large V-shaped station that orbited Seaway, a 12Mj gas giant fifteen AU from the Perry star. The station was a gas miner, utilizing massive graviton emitters on the ends of its fifty-kilometer-long arms to draw gasses off the planet below. Those gasses then pooled in a roiling mass within the center of the station's 'V'.

The gasses were held in place by a powerful grav field, and the station extracted useful isotopes before dumping the rest of the gas out in a long stream trailing behind the station.

Normally a trail like that would become a ring around the planet, and a hazard for the station itself. But a smaller outpost—called The Pup—trailed behind The Reach, shifting the waste gasses and pushing them back down to the planet below.

Jessica couldn't help but notice that while the station seemed to operate its mining systems efficiently, there were dark sections, and others surrounded by repair scaffolding that had the look of being in place for decades.

Perhaps the extortion business wasn't going that well at present.

The station's docks were situated along the first ten kilometers of each arm at the end where they met to form the V, though only the first few kilometers seemed to be in use. They consisted of a mixture of interior and exterior berths, though it looked like *Sabrina* was too large for any of the currently available interior slots— especially with the *Sexy* attached to its hull.

That was fine by Jessica. Exterior berths made it much easier to get the hell out of dodge when things went south. Which they did as often as not.

"Damnit!" Cheeky swore from the pilot's station. "You'd think that running a station ten thousand klicks above Seaway down there would be OK, but this system is the shits for navigation. There's crap everywhere. With all the extortion they have going on, they could at least tidy up their junk with the proceeds."

"I noticed you were slewing out of the pocket a bit," Jessica said from the comm station. "Wondered if you'd been enjoying the libations a bit too much before your shift."

"*Libations*, Jessica? Really? By that do you mean dippin' in the sauce, sucking back the cherries, or maybe just *booze*?"

Jessica laughed. "Libations just felt right. I'm going to bring the word back, just you wait. Before long the entire Inner Stars and half of Orion will be libatin'."

"Keep dreaming, Jess," Cargo said with a laugh. "I think maybe you've been libatin' too much lately."

Jessica gave a rueful laugh. "I think I'm just glad to be almost through this damn nebula. Two years is two too long."

"Can you imagine being one of the light huggers who work off the FTL routes?" Misha asked. "Decades of stasis to make it from one system to another."

"Yeah, but I bet those guys make serious cred," Cheeky replied. "Though I wonder what sorts go off and live inside a nebula like this."

"People who like a good night sky," Cargo replied.

"Oh, thank the big blue giants!" Cheeky exclaimed. "They've cleared the final approaches of rocks and shit. OK, thirty minutes 'til we're latched and hatched."

Cargo rose and stretched. "Good, we'll get our shit done here, and then get gone. The sooner we're out of the Perry Strait, the sooner you two will stop talking like we're in some corny vid."

Jessica looked at Cheeky, who was peering back over her shoulder. They both winked and began to laugh.

"Women," Cargo muttered as he walked off the bridge.

"What was that?" Cheeky called back.

"You heard me!" Cargo yelled as he stomped down the ladder.

Misha chuckled nervously. "What's up with him? He's been acting weird all day."

"Cargo?" Jessica asked. "He was totally hot for Brooke, but she shut him down at the airlock."

"How do you know?" Misha asked.

"Sabrina told me."

<Jessica! That was supposed to be between us girls!>

"Stars, Cargo totally needs to get laid," Cheeky said with a laugh. "I'd do it, but he gets all weird after we have sex."

"That's it!" Jessica declared. "I hereby announce the commencement of operation Fuck Cargo."

<That's a bit on the nose, don't you think?> Iris asked.

"That's not all it's going to be on." Cheeky giggled.

Jessica lowered her voice, speaking like a sports announcer. "Two stations, seven days, one crusty dude named Cargo. A pair of women have set out on a mission. A mission to get Cargo laid. It *will* be dangerous, it *will* be perilous, it *will* test their skills like nothing ever before. It—"

<Jessica. I can hear you.> Cargo's voice came into her mind, along with a very unpleasant glower.

"Who's broadcasting the bridge audio?" Cheeky asked, looking around.

<It wasn't me!> Sabrina exclaimed.

Jessica turned to Misha whose face was nearly split in two by a massive grin.

"Misha!" Cheeky yelled.

"Still think you can do it?" Misha asked with a laugh.

Jessica rose and walked over to Misha's station holding out her hand. "Care to make a bet?"

Misha looked at Jessica's dead-serious expression, and then glanced at Cheeky who was perched on the back of her chair, staring him down.

"Uh...no."

<I can still hear you all,> Cargo said.

<Me too,> Finaeus joined in. <What's this about a bet?>

*****

"You two sure like to push Cargo's buttons," Trevor said with a shake of his head as he stood at the airlock with Jessica.

"I can't help it," Jessica replied. "He's like the big older brother you just can't help needling. He's the perfect target too, he doesn't hold grudges. Next day it's like it never happened."

Trevor's shoulders heaved as he chuckled. "True that. He's like a huge duck; everything's just water off his back. Like that time I put silicon spray on all his clothes. He couldn't sit on anything for a week without sliding right off. Never even tried to get back at me."

Jessica gave a rueful sigh. "I hope we all survive this trip; we have at least eighteen years ahead of us before we get to New Canaan. I fear we're all starting to go a bit stir crazy."

"Eighteen ahead, eleven behind—since you picked me up at Virginis, that is. Can't believe we've not even hit half way on this trip. I recall you saying something like, 'we just have to find this guy named Finaeus'."

"No kidding, right? Next time Tanis and Sera say, 'So I have this little mission for you…' remind me to run."

Trevor wrapped an arm around Jessica and pulled her close. "You got it Sparkly."

"Sparkly?"

"I'm trying out new nicknames. What do you think?"

"I think that nicknames are dangerous. Eventually Misha and Finaeus work out a way to turn them against you."

"Hmm...good point."

The outer airlock finished cycling and opened up to reveal another docking wing on another station around another star. The same ole same ole.

Jessica and Trevor walked out onto the dock and looked around as the airlock closed behind them.

"I choose right," Jessica said. "Right always works better than left."

"Sure thing, Glow-girl."

"Trevor, we just talked about this."

They hadn't made it twenty paces before Jessica saw a stocky man with his arms crossed and a decidedly unfriendly look on his face. He was standing in the middle of the wide dock, staring them down with two large, well-armed and heavily armored guards on either side of him.

"Jessica Keller?" the man asked.

<I thought we registered with psudeonyms,> Jessica asked Sabrina.

<We did.>

"Uhh...nope," Jessica replied. "Name's Katarina."

"You sure?" The man asked.

"Completely. Don't you think I'd be sure of what my name is?"

The man chuckled. "You'd be surprised how many people aren't. That being said, you'll forgive me for not taking your word for it. If you'll come with me, please."

"She's not coming with you anywhere, little man," Trevor replied.

<Excellent double entendre, dear,> Jessica said privately.

<Damn, I walked right into that one.>

"Not your call, big guy," the man said. "She's coming with me to see The Perry."

"OK guys, enough," Jessica said, raising her hands. "Enough with the coming. But seriously, there's someone here called 'The Perry'?"

The man nodded. "The Perry runs the Perry System."

"Seems unnecessarily confusing," Trevor replied. "If the system is the Perry System, should you maybe call him The Perry Man? I think it would help clear things up."

The two armed guards looked at one another and one shrugged. "Kinda makes sense."

"What is wrong with you two?" The man said, frowning at Jessica and Trevor before looking at his two guards. "And you two, shut up."

"Too long in the black, I guess," Jessica said with a shrug. "Just happy to be on a station. I didn't get the pleasure of your name, by the way. Are you perhaps The Angry Zit? You kinda look like one nestled between your goons there. What with your face being so red."

<I think you may have gone too far,> Trevor said as the man began to sputter.

The man waved his hand and six autoturrets, each sporting a rather unfriendly looking railgun, dropped from the concourse's overhead.

<Shit, yeah, I guess I did. I got caught up in the moment.>

Trevor sighed. <What else is new?>

Jessica stepped forward with her hands outstretched. "I surrender. Take me to your Perry."

<Cargo?> Trevor called back to the ship. <We have a problem.>

<What?>

<Jessica's being abducted.>

<Seriously? Again? Well, get her unabducted, or get abducted *with* her, then!> Cargo's tone was more than a little exasperated.

<On it.>

"Hey!" Trevor yelled as one of the stocky man's guards placed a pair of cuffs on Jessica. "If you take her, you gotta take me too. We're a package deal."

"Awww, Trevor," Jessica said sweetly. "You say the nicest things!"

"Fine, get him too," the man grumbled.

"Yeah," Jessica grinned. "Do as Ass Pimple says."

The stocky man walked up to Jessica and backhanded her across the face. "The names Ron, kay? Ron."

"Think I can call you Assron?" Jessica asked, only to receive a fist to the stomach.

<Probably time to tone it down,> Trevor advised.

<Yeah,> Jessica replied as she wheezed. *<I think I got Ron all riled up. I did drop nano on him, though, so I'll have his Link tapped in no time.>*

THE PERRY
STELLAR DATE: 04.20.8940 (Adjusted Years)
LOCATION: Ellis Reach
REGION: Perry System, Stillwater Nebula, Perseus Arm

Ron and his two guards led Jessica and Trevor through The Reach toward the point where the two arms met at the V's point.

As they walked, Jessica took the opportunity to examine the station and its denizens. It wasn't terribly clean, but they'd been in worse—a lot worse. The most unpleasant aspect was the subtle stink of methane from the gasses drawn off the planet below.

For the most part the people looked normal, if somewhat cowed. There was little in the way of boisterous conversation; even hawkers selling food and trinkets to people coming and going down the concourse were subdued.

<How's it going out there,> Cargo asked. <We got an official notice from the station that you've been detained for questioning. Cheeky's getting ready to sneak off the ship, and I've delayed our first cargo-pickups. Not keen on letting anyone aboard right now.>

<Just getting the lay of the land. I've tapped our escort's Link. He's not talking much right now, just reported in to The

Perry, who is some guy who runs The Reach, and the entire system, it seems like,> Jessica replied as she stepped around a stack of crates containing live chickens.

<Is that a name, or a title?> Sabrina asked.

<I did some digging in their records,> Finaeus supplied. *<Looks like the current Perry is the fifth to hold that designation, so I'd go with title. This guy apparently got the job after the previous Perry planet-dived down to Seaway without an EV suit.>*

<Tough place,> Trevor commented.

"How much further?" Jessica asked. "I didn't really dress for a forced march. These heels are killing my feet."

<I thought you said with your mods, heels never hurt,> Trevor said privately.

<They don't,> Jessica replied. *<And with a-grav stabilizers, I have nary a wobble, but Assron doesn't know that.>*

<Good use of 'nary',> Trevor replied.

<Thanks. I try.>

"Sorry doll-face, not too much longer," Ron replied. "I took you the long way. Thought I'd give The Reach a little show. Remind them what happens to people who piss off the wrong people."

"Or the Ron people," Trevor said with a chuckle.

"Real funny, big guy. You two sure have mouths on you."

"You know people who don't?" Jessica asked with a laugh. "Must be inconvenient."

Ron sputtered for a moment, then shook his head and picked up the pace. "The Perry is going to have a field day with you two."

"What does that mean anyway, 'a field day'?" Jessica asked.

"Oh, for fuck's sakes. I don't get paid enough for this shit," Ron swore and started walking even faster.

<You better get it all out of your system now,> Trevor cautioned. <I imagine whoever this Perry guy is, he's not going to just take your needling.>

<I'm trying to piss Assron off enough that he starts bitching to Perry about us over the Link. I'm hopeful that they'll hint at what they took us for.>

<How's that working,> Trevor asked.

<Not good. Assron is now bitching to his mom...or wife, I'm not sure which, he's using really unspecific pronouns. Don't you hate that?>

They didn't have much longer to wait. A minute later, Ron stopped in front of a set of large, clear doors with more guards standing on either side. He tapped his foot for a few seconds, and then the doors slid open.

Ron turned and looked back at Jessica and Trevor. "Now watch your tongue in there, The Perry is not a forgiving man. Or shoot your mouth off, not that I care."

Jessica was tempted to stick her tongue out and try to look at it, but decided against it.

<What's gotten into you?> Iris asked.

<Well, there you are. I was wondering when you'd join in the fun.>

<I was piggybacking on Ron's Link to see if I could hack into any privileged networks. Responding to your inane yammering would have been too distracting.>

Jessica gave a mental snort. <My yammering's not inane…well, mostly not inane. It served a purpose.>

<To get Ron to complain to his mother?>

<I think it's his wife,> Jessica countered.

<You're clearly not paying close enough attention. It's his mother.>

Jessica paused for a moment. <Do you think maybe he's married to his mother? Does that sort of thing fly here in Perryland?>

<You're incorrigible.>

Jessica grinned at Iris's silver form in her mind. <Yes, this is true. It is impossible to corrige me.>

Once through the doors, Ron led them down a long, carpeted hall. At the end, he turned right at a broad foyer and approached another set of doors.

A pair of guards stood at the doors and pulled them wide as the group approached.

"The Perry is ready to see you," one of them said.

Jessica opened her mouth to respond, but Trevor gave her a quelling look and she pursed her lips instead.

Ron's two guards pushed them through the entrance, and Jessica looked around the room.

It was smaller than she had expected, but had a welcoming feel. The burgundy carpet was thick, the walls paneled in a dark red oak, and tall windows looked out over a vista of wooded foothills marching up to a craggy mountain range—holodisplays, of course.

There were leather couches along the walls, and some small tables before them, but the room was dominated by a huge mahogany desk, and the desk was dominated by a huge man.

<Can I say something about how modern science—you know the kind from seven thousand years ago—can help him?> Jessica asked Trevor.

<I'd really prefer that you didn't.>

Ron approached the desk and gestured to Jessica and Trevor. "Sir, I've brought them as you requested."

"I don't recall asking for a 'them'," The Perry replied in a deep base. "I just asked for her."

"I know," Ron said nervously. "But he really wanted to come…and I figured the bou—"

The Perry held up a hand and Ron stopped talking.

"So, Jessica Keller, is it? Or should I say, *Retyna Girl*."

"The who or the who?" Jessica asked. "I told your man here that I'm Katarina. This is my guy, Borus."

"You can call me Bore," Trevor said with a nod.

"Really?" The Perry asked with a mischievous smirk. "That the story you're going to stick with?"

"Unless you have a better one," Jessica replied.

The Perry clapped his hands with delight. "Oh, you're fun! Usually there's so much pleading and groveling. I like sassy for a change. Too bad I won't be able to keep you."

"Keep me?" Jessica asked

A holodisplay activated and an image appeared over The Perry's desk, rotating slowly.

Jessica groaned and placed her face in her hands. "I thought we'd never see that again."

There hovering over The Perry's desk, was Retyna Girl in an action pose with the words, 'Look out barren worlds, here comes Retyna Girl!' above her head.

"So, then," The Perry said with a toothy smile, "You *are* Jessica Keller, AKA Retyna Girl, which makes your erstwhile companion here, Trevor."

"You got us," Jessica said.

"And your ship is *not* the *Sacred Retribution*," The Perry continued. "Rather, it is the *Matron Tulip*."

<You catching all this?> Jessica asked Cargo.

<Yeah. I missed part of your last chat with Ron—they'd cut the ship off from the public nets, but Nance and Erin got around that pretty quickly. I really wonder how Retyna Girl posters got here so soon—or how they got anywhere at all.>

Jessica had wondered the same thing. *<You'd think with Marsalla gone, RHY's whole alien biology division would be done.>*

<Well,> Finaeus interjected. *<They probably sent some samples out to their corporate HQ. You also possess their technology too—perhaps the last if they were terribly unlucky.>*

Jessica wondered about that. Even if RHY hadn't preserved some strain of their Retyna product, why would they hunt her down? There was no reason to believe that RHY—or anyone else, for that matter—knew that Jessica and the team had survived *Sabrina's* destruction of the planet back in the Naga System.

Then it dawned on Jessica, and she shook her head. "Derrick."

"So you're not dumb as a plum after all," Perry said with a smirk. "Yes, Derrick has placed a rather hefty bounty on your head. He even sent ahead an incentive for us to keep an eye out for you."

"That was very thoughtful of him," Jessica replied. "I'm surprised his message beat us."

The Perry shrugged. "You're not the only ones who know about this route through the nebula. We've traded with Derrick for some time. His message said he was almost certain you'd come this way. When Brooke saw your shiny purple ass, she knew we'd hit a nice little jackpot."

"You run a whole system," Trevor said. "What could Derrick offer you that would make this worth it?"

"The Perry Strait is a complex operation. The system and the nebula are constant adversaries. Every little bit helps. Derrick, however, wasn't interested in you. He seems to want your ship. What he doesn't know is that no ship is worth what RHY would pay to get their hands back on Retyna Girl."

"How would you know what RHY would want?" Jessica asked. "You run a system in the ass crack of nowhere."

"Ever heard of jump gates?" The Perry asked. "They're a new FTL tech. RHY has some. News of their…troubles…in the Naga System traveled fast and came to us through the coreward end of the strait. Turns out you were already in their corporate reports. There was mention of the Retyna subdivision being shut down because all viable samples were lost."

<*Well, now we know that we stopped their plan to make a planet-killing bacteria,*> Iris said.

"That's a real shame," Jessica said aloud. "I bet their board was very displeased."

"Yes, they were quite upset from what I heard," The Perry said before he leaned forward and placed his elbows on his desk, rubbing his meaty hands together. "But Derrick's message had this interesting little tidbit in it. He noted that you'd been injected with the Retyna product—it's what makes your skin glow."

Awww shit, Jessica thought.

"I was, but they took it out," Jessica replied. She doubted The Perry would buy it, she had glowed faintly the entire time they had been speaking.

"Sure, yeah, keep telling yourself that," The Perry said. "So, anyway, I've already sent a message to RHY that you're alive, and that I'm willing to discuss…oh…a planet or two in trade for you. Derrick is also coming to get his hands on your ship—though I can't imagine why. He's going to kick himself when he realizes what he let slip through his fingers."

<*You know,*> Jessica said over the team's net. <*This was one of those times where getting captured to find out what the enemy wants was not a good idea.*>

<*It's rarely a good idea,*> Cargo replied.

<*This time it's been great,*> Finaeus replied. <*This is very useful. I, for one, am very happy to learn that RHY does not*

have any of their bacteria—or at least not enough to engineer their weapon.>

<What about us?> Jessica asked.

<Well, it's good to know that RHY knows about you again. Well not good that they know, but good that we know that they know,> Misha said. <Imagine if we docked at a station and they were lying in wait, ready to pick you up?>

Cargo sighed. <What do you think just happened, Misha?>

<Uh, yeah, well, I mean a real station, not some flying V in the backend of nowhere. We can take these guys, right?>

<I'm all for that,> Jessica replied. <Screw this station and whatever cargo we had for it. I'm ready to shoot our way out of here. We've got what we need.>

<I don't think that's a very good idea,> Iris replied.

<Why not?> Jessica asked. <Their head honcho is some guy named 'The Perry'. On that alone I know we can take them.>

<Look,> Iris said. <If we don't nip this in the bud here, we'll have Derrick chasing us all the way to New Canaan, spilling the beans everywhere. Not only that, but RHY is going to be looking for us. Really ruins the whole fly-under-the-radar thing we've been working so hard at.>

<You really stacked a lot of metaphors up nicely,> Finaeus said with what sounded like sincere appreciation. <I'd hardly believe you are an AI at all, Iris.>

<I blame The Dream,> she replied sourly.

<Iris makes a good point,> Cargo said. *<We need to kill Derrick, and somehow convince RHY that The Perry has led them astray.>*

<OK, so how are we going to do that?> Jessica asked.

<Umm…good question.>

Jessica brought her attention back to The Perry's office. The man had been going on about how she was a fool for docking there—which she completely agreed with. It seemed as though she and Trevor would be his guests for some time.

"So, what now?" she asked.

"Now?" A menacing grin split The Perry's face. "I suppose I should put you to use."

CHEEKY'S OUTING
STELLAR DATE: 04.20.8940 (Adjusted Years)
LOCATION: *Sabrina*
REGION: Perry System, Stillwater Nebula, Perseus Arm

<OK, I'm suited up and ready for EV,> Cheeky said over the shipnet. <You sure you've found a dead spot in their station sensor grid, Nance?>

<Yeah, Erin and I both agree. They have a maintenance scaffold sitting out near our berth and it's blocking their view of the lower aft section of the ship,> Nance replied with calm certainty.

<If I get my ass shot off, I'm holding you responsible,> Cheeky replied as she opened the ship's lower service hatch. She recalled the last time she had used this as an emergency exit. It had been back when she and Finaeus had used it to slip past the Transcend soldiers on Gisha station.

She remembered it fondly. It was the event that had started…whatever it was she and Finaeus had going on.

Cheeky peered out along the hull and gauged the distance to the maintenance scaffolding. It was at least twenty meters past the ship's starboard fusion engine. If she was careful, she could make it without using the jets on her EV suit.

After the events at the Grey Wolf Star, Cheeky had studiously avoided any EV. Any time she thought of going outside the ship, memories of slipping past the mining ring and accelerating toward the black holes filled her mind.

The fact that the suit she was wearing was little more than five millimeters of flexible polymer between her and the cold vacuum of space didn't help either.

<Easy, Cheeky,> Piya said privately. <You got this. Nothing to worry about out here.>

<Except for that very large jovian planet down there. You know, the one that will have no trouble sucking me in?>

<Not going to happen. You're just going a few meters; you're not going to lose any relative velocity. This is a piece of cake.>

A piece of cake. Right, Cheeky thought.

She wished she hadn't volunteered to go across to the station, but she knew that no one else could do it. Cargo had to stay with the ship—at some point someone would expect to speak with the captain and it would be awkward if he were on the station.

Finaeus and Misha were useless for this sort of work. Well, Finaeus could do it, but he was often indelicate. No one had even asked Nance. Stealth and smooth talking were not her thing—at least not until recent years.

No. When it was time to send in the cavalry for a rescue—or at least intel gathering—it seemed Cheeky herself was the best option.

What have we come to?

Cheeky activated the maglocks in her gloves and carefully pulled herself across the hull of the ship. She moved slowly, keeping in the shadows just in case someone peered out an observation port. When she reached the engines, Cheeky very carefully clambered over its fins before coming to the furthest point on the ship.

<*There, see that spar sticking out on the scaffolding? Aim for that. If you miss, there are two others beyond it,*> Piya advised.

<*And then?*> Cheeky asked.

<*Well, past that is the station, which is where you want to go anyway,*> Piya's voice was calm and soothing. <*Worst case scenario you alert them to your presence. You're not going to get lost in space out here.*>

<*I'm glad you're so confident.*>

<*Hey, I'm in here too. If I didn't think you could do it, I'd tell you not to.*>

Cheeky nodded. <*Good point.*>

She closed her eyes and drew in a deep breath before opening them again, taking careful aim, disabling her maglock, and pushing off from *Sabrina*.

Twenty meters. A breeze, you could do this in your sleep.

The spar approached, and Cheeky reached out for it, only to realize at the last moment that she'd forgotten to reenable her maglocks, and her glove slid off the spar.

She activated the magnets in her gloves, but it was too late. "Damnit," she whispered as she began to spin, though still on course for the next spar.

<*Do you need jets?*> Piya asked.

<*No, I've got it, if I just, stretch…. Got it!*>

<*Told you that you could do it!*> Piya exclaimed.

Cheeky clamped her second hand around the spar, and then worked her way toward one of the scaffold's main struts that was anchored to the station.

A minute later her boots were maglocked onto the station's skin and she slowly walked to the closest airlock. When she arrived, Cheeky peered through the window to see that it was empty.

Thank the stars for small miracles.

<*Time to see if Nance and Erin can remote hack this thing on a tightband,*> Cheeky said to Piya before connecting back to the ship. <*OK, I'm here and I've placed the hack terminal over the access pad.*>

<*Good,*> Nance replied. <*Give us a minute…altering their logging parameters…oh this weird stuff. What were they thinking?*>

<There, that service,> Erin said, *<shut it down and I'll reset the parameters. Good.>*

<Go for it, Cheeky. The override passcode is one-one-one.>

Cheeky chuckled. *<I can't believe they have a system that even lets you use that as a code.>*

<I think their security systems predate space flight,> Nance added. *<Or someone was just really lazy. Or both.>*

<I'll take either,> Cheeky replied as she punched in the new code and smiled with delight as the airlock door slid open. She stepped inside and scanned the airlock which also doubled as EV suit storage.

The station's suits were larger, heavy-duty affairs, all standing in recessed racks along the right side of the airlock.

"Which suit does everyone hate?" Cheeky asked softly as she looked them over.

Sure enough, there was an older suit that looked unused. She could tell because there was a cobweb between the arm and the hip. There was also a bit of a musty smell coming from inside.

"Jackpot. You're my new storage locker," she said with a smile. The outer door finished sealing, and Cheeky pulled off her helmet, and then shimmied out of her EV suit. She rolled it up and stuffed it inside the unused station suit before tucking her helmet behind it's boots.

Once she was satisfied that the helmet wasn't visible, Cheeky checked herself over. Halter top and short skirt were in place, an extra layer of sim-skin was firmly attached to the bottoms of her otherwise bare feet, and her hair looked perfect.

Time to gather some intel.

She palmed the control to open the inner door and almost collided with a tall, spindly man.

"Hey," he said, scowling down at her. "What are you doing in there?"

Cheeky recalled a name she'd seen written on tape over one of the EV suits and smiled sweetly. "I was waiting for Jerry, he told me to meet him here for a bit of hanky panky. He never showed, and I got tired of waiting. I guess he's off with someone else."

The man scowled at Cheeky. "*I'm* his someone else! Where did you meet him?"

"Uhh, at the bar?"

The man turned and stormed away, muttering angrily, "That dickhead! I'm gonna tear his ears off."

<Smooth,> Piya said. <You never even batted an eyelash.>

<You know me, Piya. I think I've used that same excuse a hundred times now.>

<Closer to two hundred, but who's counting?>

<You, apparently.>

Piya gained access to the local public network and they searched for any infrequent visitors to The Reach who bore a passing resemblance to Cheeky.

They finally found one—a woman named Arn who had been on station ten years ago, but hadn't shown up since. She looked similar enough to Cheeky, and Piya was able to lift her public tokens out of the logs.

Piya grinned as she updated their net presence to appear as Arn. <*I'm not a patch on Nance and Erin, but like they said, this place has really poor net security. I guess they don't get a lot of traffic from more advanced systems.*>

<*You've got mad skills, Piya. Sucks that we have to go by 'Arn', though. What a dumb name.*>

<*Says 'Cheeky',*> Piya replied with a smile.

<**Cheeky** *has special meaning—meaning everyone gets right away. 'Arn' just sounds like 'Arm' with a stuffed nose.*>

Piya laughed in Cheeky's mind, and then provided the route to a bar that was in the opposite direction of the angry man they had just encountered.

In the ten minutes it took to get to the bar, Cheeky concluded that Jessica had been right in the observations she'd passed back to the crew. The Reach was dull with a side of boooooring. It was like everything had no color. The people simply milled about, doing…whatever it was they were doing…with minimal effort.

She hoped the bar scene would be a little more exciting, or she was going to have a hard time getting people to talk.

The first bar they came to bore the name 'The Warped Hull'. Cheeky stepped in to find it half empty. A bit surprising, given the hour. As she looked over the décor and the menu, she wasn't surprised. The place was minimalist in both food and atmosphere.

People liked to drink in places where they could feel nestled in. Close, protected. Where everyone was just another guy or gal trying to make it through this thing called life.

Cheeky doubted that she'd be able to get anyone to talk in a place like The Warped Hull. She needed to find a seedy joint where the locals cut loose. No matter how repressed they all were under this Perry guy, people were people, and they always found a way to have a good time.

After three more strikeouts, Cheeky decided to try a place called Sally Jane's Liquor Outlet. Its listing on the nets made it look like a wholesaler of some sort, but there were also comments about what was on tap by some visitors.

<*Couldn't hurt to try, right?*> Cheeky asked Piya.

<*Sure. If that doesn't work you can always hang out a shingle.*>

<Piya!> Cheeky exclaimed with mock outrage. *<I don't do sex for money. That's crass! It devalues the whole thing.>*

<I love you Cheeky, you're a glorious mess.>

<I'm not above a tip, though.>

When they reached Sally Jane's Liquor Outlet, Cheeky saw a rather sedate looking storefront—closed this late at night—but there was a narrow corridor running alongside it, and she walked inside. Sure enough, she could hear the thrum of music, and the sound of voices raised over the din.

Finally.

A door stood at the end of the corridor and Cheeky reached out to palm the access panel when it slid aside and a couple lurched out.

She realized that one of them was the man she had met at the airlock and quickly turned her head as the pair stumbled out into the corridor.

If this place was 'the bar' then she had finally struck gold.

The music wasn't as loud as Cheeky had expected, but as she slipped past the couple, she found herself in a small room with a rather lanky man blocking a second door.

"Password?" he asked in a bored tone of voice.

"The rubber duck quacks at midnight?" Cheeky asked with a grin.

"Not even close."

"Uh...Perry's a sonofabitch, but he's *our* sonofabitch?"

The man laughed at that one, but still shook his head.

Cheeky tapped her chin and looked up at the overhead. "How about: I fuck for drinks?"

That one got a loud bark of laughter from the man and he shook his head. Cheeky began to think of another, but he leaned over and opened the door.

"You're funny and ready for fun. I like it. You're in."

The music hit her like a wall, right along with the smell. It wasn't bad, per se, but there was a certain odor a place got when a hundred drinks sloshed on the floor, right along with the sweat from the hundred people holding them. Cram it all into one place and it was like humanity's third-watch perfume.

Cheeky reveled in it. Finally. This was her kind of place.

<OK, Piya, so we're here to find someone who works for The Perry so we can get them to talk about his operation, and what we can expect him to do. Got any candidates?>

<I see a couple in The Reach guard uniforms over there,> Piya said, highlighting a pair of women who were arm-wrestling with a slew of drinks around them.

<They scare me. Next?>

<Hmm…that guy over there is wearing the same uniform that Brooke had on. Maybe he's a good one to start with.>

Cheeky spotted the man. He had long red hair, a bit of an aquiline nose, and full lips. His shoulders were broad, but he didn't look like he was modded up to attain the look.

<He'll do.>

He didn't do.

The man was waiting for his wife and wasn't about to risk her ire chatting with Cheeky. Eventually, Cheeky gave up and sat at the bar. She ordered a Serenading Peacock, which they all seemed to call Sex on the Moon in the Stillwater Nebula.

<I'm a failure, Piya. Have I lost my charm?>

<One bar out of ten thousand where you can't get someone to open up is hardly a failure.>

Cheeky shook her head. <No, there was that other one too…out in Deneb, remember?>

<Ohh…where they did that thing to you that we don't talk about.>

Cheeky took a sip of her drink. <Don't remind me…. How was I supposed to know that only blue-skinned people were allowed to talk in that club? No one expects a rule like that. Especially for it not to be posted.>

<It was. Right above the bar.>

<Yeah, but the bar was on the far side of a hundred really hot people. I don't think I even made it that far.>

"You look like it's not your night," the bartender said as he wiped up a spill.

"Not my best, no," Cheeky replied.

"Name's Bill," the bartender said as he began to prepare a drink for an order that was just screamed at him from across the room. "Been a rough night here too. Sally was supposed to be around to help me, but The Perry called her up to his place for some sort of shindig he's having."

"Ch—Arn," Cheeky said with a smile

"Charn?" Bill frowned. "Not sure I've ever heard that name before."

"Sorry, had something caught in my throat. Arn, the name's Arn."

Bill looked at her like he still wasn't sure he'd heard correctly and then shrugged. "Well, Arn, you want another Sex on the Moon? We close up in an hour and when I make last call it'll get busy for a bit."

"In that case, why don't you make two?"

Bill looked her up and down. "You sure you can handle it?"

Cheeky chuckled. "Bill, I'm sure I *can't*. Load me up."

SLOP & DINNER
STELLAR DATE: 04.21.8940 (Adjusted Years)
LOCATION: Waste Reclamation Center 12A, Ellis Reach
REGION: Perry System, Stillwater Nebula, Perseus Arm

"Stars! Repulsive as The Perry is, I think I'd rather have fucked him than do this," Jessica said as she opened up the hatch on the next filtration tank and nearly gagged at the smell. "I mean…I can't imagine these things have been cleaned in…ever."

Trevor hauled the pressure washer over with one hand, the other covering his nose. "What's really insulting is that they think they only need two guards to watch us."

Jessica glanced back at the pair of guards watching them. During yesterday's manual labor, they had been watched by the same two men who had escorted them up from the docks. Today there was a new set. A man and a woman who seemed more interested in talking to each other about a sim game they were into than watching their charges.

<I've calculated seventeen different ways I can take them out,> Jessica said. <This whole place is amateur hour. I sure hope that RHY and Derrick don't take long to get here. I just might have to stage a coup on principle alone.>

<I don't think Cargo would like that plan,> Trevor cautioned.

Jessica snorted. <Cargo doesn't like most of my plans—except the one that got us off Gisha Station back at the Grey Wolf System. He **liked** that plan, and look where it got us?>

<Well, the alternative was in some Transcend black site with our innards mixed with our outards.>

Jessica glanced at Trevor as he connected the water source to the pressure washer. <I don't even understand what that means.>

<You know, torture, where they pull out intestines and stuff?> Trevor made a gesture to show guts being pulled out and Jessica shook her head.

<No one does that anymore. Too ineffective.>

<Never underestimate how fast someone will start talking when you show them the food they ate last night while it's still inside them.>

Jessica felt bile rise in her throat. <Seriously! Trevor! That's horrible. Did you ever do that? How could you have done that and never told me?>

<I never did. Didn't have the stomach for it. Badump tshhhh.> His mental avatar made a rim-shot.

Jessica groaned. <Stars in heaven, two years away from the kids and your dad humor still hasn't let up.>

<It's a chronic disease. I'm afflicted for life.>

Jessica pulled her hazsuit's hood over her head and sealed it. Then she checked the seal and had Trevor triple check. Once he nodded that she was well and truly protected from the horrors she was about to face, Jessica climbed into the tank.

<This is what I get for marrying a man with shoulders the size of a house,> she said. <I get to go into the disgusting tank and spray off the…whatever.>

<Somehow I think this one minor inconvenience doesn't offset everything else,> Iris said with a laugh.

<Minor? I wish you had a body. I'd make you do this. I can smell it through the hazsuit.>

<No you can't. That's just your imagination. Besides, if I had a body, it wouldn't be organic. So stuff that's 'gross' wouldn't bother me. Stars, have you seen where my physical body sits? Human brains are kinda yicky on the inside.>

"I'll show you 'yicky'," Jessica muttered as she began to spray the strange green and yellow slime off the inside of the tank. It ran down the sides and pooled at the bottom in a sloppy mass. Jessica had to blast it with the pressure washer repeatedly to get the stuff to break up enough to go down the drain.

<Oh man,> Trevor said from outside the tank. <This one smells even worse than the last. There're still six more to do too.>

<I don't want to **hear** about it, Trevor,> Jessica said, her teeth gritted tightly.

<I'd join in your coup if it meant that I didn't ever have to smell this again,> Trevor replied.

<Oh yeah?> Jessica asked. <How many soldiers do you think The Perry has. Like loyal ones?>

Trevor grunted. <Not sure. Iris, you've probably hacked your way through their entire network here by now. How's it shake out?>

<You sure you want to do this? We're supposed to lay low. Taking out The Perry won't be hard—probably—but then we might have to run this stupid station for months.>

<Months? We'll have to **run** it for months? How is that worse than slopping out these tanks for months? Sign me up.>

<Trevor,> Iris said with a worried tone. <I think we should consider it, if only so that Jessica doesn't lose her mind and do something drastic.>

A second later, Jessica let out a blood curdling scream. <Sweet stars, what is **that**, and how did it get in here?!>

* * * * *

"If you don't like it here, why do you stay?" Cheeky asked Bill as they relaxed on his couch, sharing a bottle of wine after their most recent round of lovemaking.

Bill took a sip of wine before replying in a tone that implied she should already know the answer. "Well, there's The Perry."

"The guy who runs things around here?" Cheeky asked. "Do you owe him money or something?"

Bill chuckled. "Not exactly like that, no. I guess you really don't know, do you?"

Cheeky shrugged. "Ellis Reach is just one of a hundred stations I pass through—well, maybe a thousand, actually. I don't really make it a point to learn about each one's boss man/woman/whatever."

"Huh...well, did you hear how the previous Perry died?"

"Something about sucking vacuum on the way down to Seaway, right?" Cheeky asked.

Bill nodded. "Yeah the new Perry—his name's actually Simon—pushed him out an airlock with a rocket strapped to his back. Or at least that's how the story goes. Anyway, Simon, the new Perry, didn't really want to go the way of his last few predecessors, so he has a self-destruct system set up somewhere on the station. Rumor has it that it's on a deadman's switch, or at the very least something he has to contact every so often."

Cheeky pulled a face as she thought about that. "Sounds like a really shitty setup. But seems like all the more reason to get the heck out of here. From the pictures I've seen, The Perry looks none too healthy. He's probably not long for this life."

Bill let out a long sigh before downing his wine. "Yeah, not really encouraging for those of us who are stuck here."

"Back to that," Cheeky said. "You're not stuck here. Ships come and go all the time."

"Not an option," Bill replied. "There's a beacon in the system that we can all pick up no matter where we are. We receive the beacon, we're OK. We lose contact with the beacon for more than a few minutes and we lose our heads."

Cheeky sat up straight. "What? Seriously? Bomb in the head? Isn't that the sort of thing you find in a bad vid?"

Bill gave a sour laugh. "Well, The Perry must have watched a lot of those. After he announced how the station would blow if he died, a lot of folks did just what you suggested...got the hell out of here. The Perry wasn't so keen on that, so he took all of us working-class schleps and loaded us up with our little surprises."

"Damn," Cheeky said with a whistle. "That's barbaric."

"Welcome to the Perry Strait."

<Piya, can you relay this info to Cargo? He needs to know it. Probably Jessica and Trevor too.>

<You got it. I have a drop set up with Erin and Sabrina. Sending this conversation in.>

* * * * *

Cargo closed off the latest demand from the station to disembark and surrender the ship. So far it was all bluster, just a prelude to a discussion about exchanging Jessica as a hostage—which would just be a ruse to get them off the ship.

They still had a day or two before things actually escalated.

"This is a dumb plan," Cargo said around a mouthful of potatoes. "I mean…not our worst by a long stretch, but how long are we going to have to wait? If Derrick shows up first, he's going to tell The Perry to take our ship. Then we fight back and then what?"

"Well, we'll either escape, or take the station," Nance said. "Probably escape. Station taking really isn't our thing."

"But how does that help us with RHY?" Finaeus asked. "If we escape, they'll just chase after us. But if we take the station…"

"This would be a sweet station to control," Misha added. "All the tariffs and tolls they collect gotta make a person riiiich."

"We're not moving in," Cargo replied with a glower. "But I wonder if we *should* take the station now. It's big, but it's not heavily populated. Maybe ten-thousand people aboard right now."

<Ten thousand is a lot,> Sabrina said. <And there's no central AI here for us to convince to help. Though they do have a few aboard. More than a lot of places we've come to out here.>

<OK, but their security is garbage,> Hank replied. <I saw what you two did, Erin and Nance. You walked right through it.>

<It was child's play,> Erin replied. <I suppose we could work out how to take control of this place, shut it down on a night cycle, remove The Perry, undock people we don't like, and wait for RHY to show.>

"Like Chittering Hawk all over again," Cargo mused. "I'm not normally the one for the risky play, but that would make it easier to fake out RHY when they show up—if we control the narrative, that is."

<Oh...wrinkle in the plan,> Sabrina reported. <Our boy Perry has a deadman's switch on some sort of self-destruct for the station.>

"You're kidding, right?" Finaeus asked. "What is this? Some ancient vid with Captain Evil or something?"

"I liked those vids," Cargo replied.

<Then we have a serious problem,> Erin said.

"What—I mean we're not trying to kill the guy yet," Nance said.

<Well,> Erin began. <*Iris passed a message that Jessica and Trevor were going to take out The Perry. I was going to bring it up, but you all seemed to be in agreement that we should take the station, so I didn't want to interrupt.*>

"Seriously?" Misha asked.

"Yeah, Erin, that's the sort of thing you need to share!"

<*Well, I just found out forty-nine seconds ago. Not like I sat on it for hours.*>

"So they're just going to kill him and take over?" Cargo asked. He couldn't believe Jessica would do something so reckless. Well, now that he thought about it, he could. Usually she shared her reckless plans, let him get angry about them, and then went off and executed them anyway.

<*I think that's the gist of her plan, yes,*> Erin said. <*I'm just the messenger here. It could work—if it wasn't for the deadman's switch, it probably **would** work. I think killing the prior leader is how succession works on The Reach.*>

"Great. It's a solid plan in principle." Cargo's tone was terse. "Can you tell them to stop, though?"

<*Already on it,*> Erin replied. <*We've been using a dead drop to stay on the down low, though. I'll try to reach her directly.*>

"Please do," Finaeus said. "Getting blown up isn't on the menu tonight."

* * * * *

Jessica walked into The Perry's office with the two guards at her back. She was surprised the boss-man was open to seeing her so soon and wondered if he'd sent her and Trevor to clean the tanks as some sort of special incentive.

"I heard that you didn't like being useful," The Perry said with a sly grin.

Jessica heard Trevor enter the room behind her and held back a smile. For some reason, The Perry just didn't seem to think they were threatening.

She related that to Iris and the AI replied, <You know that means this dork has to have some defense he thinks he can beat us with, right?>

<Yeah, but I can't figure out what it is. We've suffused this room with nano. There are four hidden turrets, an EMP emitter, and the gun he has under his desk.>

<Plus the guards,> Iris said.

<Yeah, but they have shitty helmets. Trevor can take them.>

Iris sighed. <If you hadn't already used too much of your remaining formation material making nano to clean your pores

after getting through those tanks, you'd have enough to lock their armor up.>

<Trevor, you worried about the guards at all?> Jessica asked.

<Nope,> Trevor replied, a broad grin in his eyes. *<Their visors don't cover their whole faces. Makes em nice and punchable.>*

<You're still missing something,> Iris replied.

<She's right,> Trevor said. *<This is way too easy.>*

As Jessica had been speaking with Trevor and Iris, she had also been exchanging barbs with The Perry. "I think there's a way I could be a lot more useful," Jessica said as she leaned over his desk, smiling wickedly.

"Oh yeah," The Perry asked.

"As The Perry—"

Jessica was halted by Iris crying out in her mind, *<Stop!>*

"—'s personal assistant."

"My personal assistant?" The Perry asked with a snort. "You're just some bimbo model that ran off with RHY's tech. What can you assist with?"

<What the hell, Iris?> Jessica asked.

<He has a deadman's switch on him…or in him. I can't find a signal, though. Unless it's encrypted in his standard Link hookup.>

<Damn,> Jessica replied. <Then how do you know it's there?>

<Cheeky found out, passed the intel along.>

Jessica took a deep breath as she tried to think of a way to back out of the situation. "Well...I've done a lot of stuff as a bimbo model. I know how to make a man happy."

The Perry snorted. "I'm already happy."

"I could make you happier."

Trevor made a gagging sound over the Link.

<Sorry hon, just have to figure out where he sends his I'm-still-breathing signal from,> Jessica replied.

"You're not really my kinda girl," The Perry said. "But I appreciate the gesture."

<What? I'm everyone's kinda girl!> Jessica exclaimed privately.

<Apparently not,> Trevor chuckled. <Thank the stars. You really would need to clean out the pores after that.>

<It wasn't like I was going to sleep with him,> Jessica replied.

<Thank all that glows in the night.>

Jessica decided to try a different tack. "I'm a really good cook."

"Oh yeah?" The Perry's eyes lit up. "How good?"

"I can cook you a meal that will make you think you're in heaven," Jessica said. "Steak, marinated in a special sauce of my own creation, seared, wrapped in bacon—and that's just the appetizer."

"You have bacon?" Perry asked, his eyes lighting up.

"Yeah, on our ship," Jessica said with a nod. "I'd love to make some for you."

Perry's visage grew cloudy. "Your friends on your ship have not been cooperative. Derrick said that he wants the ship unharmed, but I'm getting tired of playing games with your captain…shipment, or whatever his name is. So far you being a hostage has kept him from doing anything rash, though. He must like you."

"If you'll allow me, I can send him a message," Jessica said. "He'll send over some food if he thinks it's for me. I'm on a special diet."

"Of steak and bacon?" Perry asked, his tone dubious.

"Keeps the girls full," Jessica said as she cupped her breasts.

The Perry snorted. "And your ass from the looks of it. We'll have to inspect it when it comes over, but I'm willing for you to lie about your tits and ass if it gets me steak and bacon."

"Great," Jessica said. "Then I'll hit the kitchen and get started. I'll need Trevor too. He's my assistant."

"Yeah, sure," The Perry said and waved them off.

*****

<So what was that in the note about your special diet?> Trevor asked.

<Formation material for more nano,> Jessica replied. <I don't have enough to hit Perry, find his deadman's switch, and take him out before he realizes what's going on. I need to fill him with the stuff first, then trigger it to do its job.>

Trevor nodded as he walked at her side toward The Perry's private kitchen—just down the hall from his office. <There's a lot of Perry to fill. What if you don't find the signal?>

<Not sure...I could maybe put him into a coma. That should work.>

<**Should** being the operative term,> Iris added.

<We'll play it by ear. Worst case scenario, he gets a good meal and I spend time outside of a hazsuit and away from those tanks. Starting to understand why Nance doesn't want to ever come out of hers.>

The kitchen was well equipped and clean. The fridge and larder were full, and in addition to the standard selection of spices, there were many neither Jessica nor Trevor had ever heard of.

While they waited for the meat to arrive, the pair worked quickly, getting the kitchen ready for the meal prep. Jessica was reclining at the table and Trevor was putting on a pot of coffee when Ron came in.

"Got your special delivery here," he said and waved in a guard carrying a crate to set it on the table. "You finally figured out the way to the big man's heart: food. He doesn't like boys or girls, just his next meal."

"Was kinda staring right at me," Jessica said with a laugh.

Ron chuckled. "Course, if he doesn't like your cooking, things'll go badly for you. He goes through a lot of chefs. Killed the last one a few days back. That's why there's no one else in here."

"Shit," Trevor muttered. "That's a man who takes his food seriously."

"You have no idea," Ron said with a grin as he turned and left. "Good luck!"

The guard set the crate on the table and then left the room, leaving Jessica and Trevor with just the two guards who had been with them all day.

"Want some coffee?" Trevor asked.

The two looked at one another and shrugged. "Why not," one replied.

Trevor poured two cups and set them at the table, then placed a tray with cream and sugar on it. One of the guards pulled out a scanner and checked over the drinks.

"Not that we don't trust you," he said. "Well, it *is* that we don't trust you."

Trevor shrugged. "I don't blame you."

The guard's scanners came up empty, and they both doctored their drinks the way they liked and took a sip.

Two minutes later they were out.

<*Test one complete. Their scanning tech can't detect our nano,*> Jessica said with a grin as she unpacked the meat and handed it to Trevor. Then she looked over the crate.

<*I think the formation material **is** the crate,*> Iris suggested.

Jessica pulled back her sleeve and touched her forearm to the case. Sure enough, the assimilator on her arm registered it as formation material and drew it in.

<*Don't really need this much,*> Jessica said. <*It'll make me fat.*>

<*You weren't really specific about what you needed. You could make some guns or knives or something too.*>

Jessica looked around at the kitchen. <*Lot of knives in here, and there are guns on the guards. Never know, though, we'll find a use for it.*>

The pair spent the next hour preparing a meal consisting of flame-grilled medallions of beef wrapped in strips of honey-cured streaky bacon and a mushroom and whole pepper jous. To accompany the succulent meat, they included a salad of steamed broccolini and baby asparagus tossed in a sweet pomegranate and mustard dressing.

After a bit of wrangling, with Trevor arguing the merits of balancing all meat dishes with a side of garlic-drenched potatoes, they added roasted garlic and rosemary smashed potatoes in a garlic-butter and white wine sauce.

A meal fit for a king.

* * * * *

Cheeky walked through The Reach's long corridors, heading toward the point of the V where The Perry's offices lay. She'd spent a little more time with Bill, trying to ferret out where the self-destruct system may be, but the bartender had had no idea.

<I'm tempted to dismiss this whole self-destruct thing as a hoax,> Cheeky said as they turned onto the concourse that ran toward The Perry's offices.

<I'm not so sure,> Piya replied. <I should say...I'm not convinced either way, but I did find something interesting as I've been hunting through their maintenance logs.>

<Oh yeah?> Cheeky asked with a chuckle. <What's up? I always love a good maintenance log.>

<You're a riot, Cheeks,> Piya replied drily. <OK, so there are notes in here about how The Perry never leaves his office

area, mainly it's workers bitching that they always have to work around him.>

Cheeky shrugged. <From what I've seen on the vids, he's a big guy, not the type for an evening stroll.>

<Right, but if you were a megalomaniac whose only real method of control was the threat of death to everyone around you, what would you not do?>

Cheeky smiled as understanding dawned on her. <I wouldn't go far from the bomb.>

<Preeeecisely.>

<So you're saying that wherever the bomb is—or whatever it is— it's in his offices,> Cheeky said.

<You just said it's and is so many times I have no idea what you mean, but if you mean that it's in his offices, then yes, I agree.>

<Harsh, Piya. Harsh.>

Cheeky slowed as she neared the larger doors leading into The Perry's offices. There were heavily armored guards both without and within. She could probably use nano—people on The Reach seemed to have almost no defense against advanced nano—to take some of them out, but not all.

<Sooooo, you know how I've been looking at the maintenance logs?> Piya asked with a sly smile.

<Yes, we just talked about your favorite pastime.>

<You know it, Cheeks, saving your ass one log review at a time. Anyway, a station with good security has advanced systems for identity management and access control. No shared creds, no simple codes, private keys, block-chain tech, right?>

<Yeah, that's how we run Sabrina.>

Piya nodded in Cheeky's mind. <Right, but people here don't give a shit. The Perry has bombs in their heads to keep them on station—or he tells them he does. I'm not convinced they all have them.>

<Annnnyway.>

<Right. Well, the maintenance techs haven't bothered creating new accounts for people to do work on various systems.>

<They use shared tokens?> Cheeky asked, her tone rising in pitch from professional outrage. Everyone knew using shared tokens was a fantastic way to come back from shore leave to find your starship stolen.

<Even better. They're noted in a master 'info' ticket in their tracking system.>

<What the actual fuck?> Cheeky exclaimed.

<Yeah, we can't tell Erin and Nance. Their collective heads will explode,> Piya said with a rueful chuckle.

<No kidding. So I assume all this means is you found a back door, and you have the codes.>

<Yeah, took a bit to get there, but I figured you'd appreciate knowing how.>

Cheeky sent a warm feeling to Piya. <I always appreciate you, hon. You're my better half.>

* * * * *

Trevor offered each of the guards standing in The Perry's office a travel mug filled with the special coffee—albeit with a longer delay in place—while Jessica set the tray of food in front of The Perry.

"Woman, this smells amazing. For a glowing purple bimbo, you sure can do something magical."

<That's starting to get on my nerves,> Jessica said privately to Iris and Trevor.

<You may be a glowing purple bimbo,> Trevor said with a laugh, <but you're **my** glowing purple bimbo.>

<What about me?> Iris asked. <I thought I was your silver copycat bimbo.>

<I should never have said anything,> Trevor replied.

Jessica watched as The Perry picked up his cutlery and began to dig into the meal. She had a moment of silence for the amazing meal that he shoveled into his mouth as though it was the only way to stop his body from instantly imploding.

Iris gave a low whistle. <OK, I'm not organic, but that's even grossing me out. Somehow, it's worse than the tank.>

Jessica nearly gagged. <Stars, Iris! I can't handle thinking of those tanks and this…this…disaster in front of me at the same time!>

<Sorry. I have to admit I was a bit curious if I could get you to lose your lunch,> Iris replied.

<I get the distinct impression that you two aren't taking this seriously enough,> Trevor interjected.

<Trevor,> Jessica replied. <The last crisis we faced involved raising sixteen children and then setting them loose with the most powerful weapons we've ever seen to destroy a massive fleet of Orion Guard ships. Doesn't this feel almost…I don't know…anticlimactic by comparison?>

<Unless Perry climaxes,> Iris said with a wicked smile.

<Oh shit, I might lose it now,> Jessica groaned.

<OK, I've hit critical mass. He's sucked in a half a kilogram of nano at this point,> Iris reported.

Jessica swallowed her disgust. <Alright, let's see what makes this man tick.>

* * * * *

Cheeky stood at the unmarked grey door and brought up the access code Piya had located: 'Simon is a Fucking Asshole'.

<These guys are real creative,> she thought before punching it in. <You ready.>

<I'm an AI, Cheeky. I'm always ready.>

<I feel like that could be the tagline for a movie,> Cheeky said while grinning. <OK. Here goes.>

She hit the send key, and without a moment's hesitation, the door popped open.

"Well, I'll be damned," she muttered and stepped inside.

Cheeky found herself in a long corridor with several doors along either side and crept down it slowly, sending out a passel of probes to check for any surveillance systems, or approaching people.

<Check that door to the left,> Piya said. <If the information I have is right, there should be a staircase.>

Cheeky approached the door and pulled it open to reveal a mop closet with a pair of meter-high cleaning bots backed into charging stations.

<Fail, Piya.>

<Doing the best I can. These guys aren't super organized. Try the next door.>

Cheeky walked to the next one and found herself in a store room filled with chairs and desks.

<This too does not look like a stairwell.>

<Go back to that other closet, I'm curious about something.>

Cheeky returned to the mop closest and closed the door after herself. <*You thinking there's some sort of hidden hatch in here or something?*>

<*Yeah, there's gotta be. Maybe behind the bots?*>

Cheeky tried to activate the first bot and it wouldn't turn on, so she wrestled it off its charging station. The moment she did, the thing came to life and started banging into the door, trying to get out.

"Shit!" Cheeky swore. She tried to turn the thing off, but saw that its main power switch was already in the off position. <*I can't believe this stupid station hasn't fallen into Seaway already.*>

<*Just let it out,*> Piya suggested.

Cheeky pushed the bot back with a foot and then opened the door wide. The bot rushed out and almost knocked over a woman walking by.

"Hey! Whaaat the—? Who are you?"

Cheeky wiped her forehead and smiled. "I got sent down to fix the bots, but that thing went psycho on me!"

"Get out of there! Those bots don't work," the woman admonished. Her long red pony tail shook angrily as she gestured at Cheeky to come out of the closet.

"I know. Why do you think I got sent down here to fix them?"

"Who are you?" the woman asked, stepping closer to reach for Cheeky.

"Arn. Here to fix the bots, like the one you just let get away."

"Arm?"

"No Arn. Oh for fucksakes." Cheeky grabbed the woman's outstretched hand and pulled her into the closet, then slammed the redhead's temple into a shelf and then drove a fist into her solar plexus.

The woman crumpled, and Cheeky reached behind her head and touched the woman's neck.

"I don't know how we managed before we had the *Intrepid*'s fancy nano," Cheeky said.

<Thompson would have killed her,> Piya replied.

<Sssssss, you spoke of he-who-shall-not-be-named!>

<Sorry,> Piya said and then highlighted the panel behind the cleaning bot's charging station. <Look, it's loose. That's our way in.>

<And by it, I assume you mean where the bomb is.>

<Yeeeup.>

Cheeky prised the panel open—which proved to be an easy task as it was on hinges. Behind was a down-sloping narrow passage which led into a room five meters across and five deep.

The moment she laid eyes on what rested in the center of the space, Cheeky began to sweat.

<Piya, get Nance and Erin realtime, we're going to need their help.>

* * * * *

The Perry was in mid-chew when he stopped, and his eyes grew wide.

"What…!"

Jessica glanced back at Trever, who pushed over the pair of wobbling guards, and smiled. "Looks like we make a *killer* meal."

"How?" Perry gasped as he clutched his throat and gagged. "We scanned it…"

"Your tech sucks, Perry," Jessica replied. "Maybe if you spent your money on something other than expensive chefs who you kill when they displease you, you'd have spotted the metric crunkload of nano that we just got you to eat."

Perry's look of fear turned into one of sly rage. "If you're trying to kill me, it won't go well. I have…a bomb," he rasped.

"Not trying to kill you," Jessica replied as she sat on the edge of his desk. "My AI, Iris, is just looking through your…body…to find out where your transmitter is. Once she finds it and we replicate its signal, *then* we kill you."

"No," Perry said with a wicked grin. "I kill you."

He reached under his desk, and Jessica dove to the side, thinking he was going for his gun, but he just pushed on something and then sat back, wheezing softly.

"There, it's done. See you in hell."

Jessica rushed around his desk to see a mechanical lever that had been pulled down.

"A lever?" she exclaimed. "Damnit!"

<*He had an internal signal too. I've replicated it just in case. You can kill him.*>

Jessica sighed. She didn't even care enough to do that. <*Just knock him out.*>

<*Jessica, you there?*> Cargo asked. <*Cheeky's with the bomb, and it's a doozy! It's activating!*>

<*Crap, Trevor, we need to get out of here!*>

<*Don't bother,*> Cargo said. <*It's a thousand kilograms of antimatter. Cheeky's working on it with Nance and Erin over the Link, but it's on a five-minute timer!*>

<*A **thousand**?! What did he think he needed to do? Blow up Seaway as well?*>

"I guess we know where his money went," Trevor said.

Jessica shook her head and leaned against the wall. "Well, shit."

THE BOMB
STELLAR DATE: 04.21.8940 (Adjusted Years)
LOCATION: Beneath The Perry's offices, Ellis Reach
REGION: Perry System, Stillwater Nebula, Perseus Arm

<Holy crap, it just started drawing particulate matter into the secondary chamber!> Cheeky exclaimed.

<OK,> Nance said calmly. <That's the regular matter. When it gets a thousand kilos in there, it's going to use flash injectors to intermix the matter and antimatter.>

<Nance. I know how an antimatter bomb works. Same as our AP drive...just a fuck-ton more antimatter. Once the injectors fire, the containment field gets obliterated—then the rest of the antimatter mixes with regular matter, and goodbye Ellis Reach.>

<Well, yeah,> Nance replied. <Of course, just the small amount that will get pushed in by the injectors is enough to blow The Reach. This thing is overkill with a side of overkill.>

<I don't see how to stop the injector process,> Piya said. <It's in a self-contained system that had been physically cut off when the countdown started. Getting at it would mean breaking containment on the antimatter.>

<Stars,> Cheeky muttered. <Fucking Perry had shitty everything else. Why couldn't he have bought the discount antimatter bomb?>

<OK, Cheeky, I need you to let me through,> Nance said.

<Let me through what?>

Nance's words were calm and reassuring. <You. I need to pass through you to do this.>

<Nance, you can't do that. You're a person, not an AI,> Piya said.

<I can, I've been studying the AHAP bot you used on Serenity. I was curious how it managed a full transference, and I worked it out. I can do it with a person if they allow it.>

<Uhh…>

<Cheeky,> Nance said sharply, <We're all going to die in two minutes and seven seconds. So we can die, or we run the risk that I fuck you up a bit but we all live. You pick.>

Cheeky bit her lip. <Piya?> she asked privately.

<I don't want to die, Cheeky.>

Cheeky drew a deep breath. <OK, Nance. Come in.>

A strange, light seemed to fill Cheeky and she felt a surge of energy—she could sense Nance in her mind, and then suddenly Nance *was* her mind and she was just an observer in her own body.

Then everything went black.

When Cheeky came to, Jessica was holding her and whispering something in her ear…she couldn't make it out, but she picked out the word safe. She tasted iron in her mouth. No, not iron, blood.

Then Cheeky passed out again.

PERINA
STELLAR DATE: 04.23.8940 (Adjusted Years)
LOCATION: The Perina's offices, Ellis Reach
REGION: Perry System, Stillwater Nebula, Perseus Arm

"Ron, if you call me *The* Perina one more time I'm going to punch you in the mouth until it falls off," Jessica said from behind her large mahogany desk. "Now, how is the process going with the bombs?"

Ron swallowed and worked his jaw for a moment. "Uh, well, most of them are fake, as it turns out, but some were real. I guess enough to work as an incentive."

"Enough to make the medics careful too, I suppose."

"Yes th—uh Perina."

Jessica hated the fact that she had to adopt a stupid title after deposing Perry—who wasn't dead, just in prison. However, she couldn't go by her name if the plan was to convince RHY that she had never been there. She could have picked something else, but the populace—who seemed very happy to have the previous Perry gone—started calling her Perina right off the bat.

The people of The Reach were very accommodating, their general efficiency improving almost overnight. The first task Jessica set them to was removing all record of

Sabrina having ever been in the system. The ship was then moved to an internal docking bay.

Sabrina wasn't happy about it, she said the station gave her the willies, as it contained too much antimatter. Jessica didn't feel much better about it—especially since it was just ten meters below her.

"OK, Ron, that's good, I suppose. No one should get sloppy. How many people left to go?"

"We still have seven thousand, though the medics think they know how to find people with the real ones now, so they're doing them first."

"Good. And the *Cloud Singer*, is it still scheduled to dock in an hour?"

"Yes, Perina, on schedule."

"Good," Jessica said as she rose. "I'll be there ten minutes early for our little surprise."

"I'm looking forward to it," Ron said while rubbing his hands.

"Oh yeah?" Jessica asked. "Derrick piss you off royally as well?"

"Well, he's a condescending bastard, and he has that weird grey skin. I can't abide grey skin. Makes people look like robot zombies."

Jessica laughed. "You know, Ron, I think you and I actually agree on something."

"Stars, don't tell anyone," Ron replied and turned to leave the office.

"Hey, Ron," Jessica called after him.

"Yeah?" Ron asked, looking back over his shoulder.

"You're doing a good job. Keep it up."

"Great. Thanks."

<He's so grumpy,> Jessica said to Iris once Ron was gone.

Iris gave a short laugh. <Jess, you threaten to hit him each time you meet with him.>

<Do I?>

<Yeah. Every time.>

<I guess he just has one of those faces.>

Jessica walked out of her office and took a dock car to *Sabrina*'s berth. As the car carried her through the station, people waved and called out in greeting. Jessica smiled and returned the waves. It was as though it were an entirely new place, even the lighting seemed brighter than when she'd first come aboard.

Sabrina was only a kilometer away, and just a few minutes later, Jessica arrived at the docking bay, spoke with a few of the station's people for a minute, and then begged off to go onto the ship.

"You're Imperial Perinaness!" Cargo greeted her with a smirk as she stepped into the main hold.

"Stars, not you too, Cargo. I can't wait to get out of here."

<Liar, you're loving it.>

<Hush, Iris, I'm bonding with Cargo.>

"Me too. Now that these people aren't all glum and under The Perry's control, they're getting a little wild."

Jessica nodded. "I know. I had to up patrols to make sure there wasn't any looting."

"Good call on establishing the Antimatter Fund, though," Cargo said. "That gives everyone a piece of the pie if they all work together."

"Once Nance gets that thing properly dismantled, and siphons off all the antimatter."

"She'll figure it out," Jessica said. "She's really come into her own these past few years."

Cargo nodded. "Sure has." He paused, his expression troubled. "So if we get Derrick—which I imagine we will—what do we do with him? He knows too much."

Jessica looked down at her gently glowing hands as they interwove tightly. "We're going to do what we have to do, Cargo."

"Murder?"

"Execution."

"What's the difference?" Cargo asked.

Jessica sighed. This was not the time to have this debate—granted she couldn't think of a time when she *would* want to have it. "At present, I'm the Per—I run this station. Derrick's broken a number of laws here in the past, but always weaseled his way out. I can try, convict, and execute him based on those past infractions."

"Doesn't feel right," Cargo said with a shake of his head. "I know we can't just lock him up, or let him go—not unless we want to have a few dozen more situations like this happen in the future."

"And that's where we are, Cargo. Derrick wants to use, exploit, and probably kill us. We can't have him loose, or for there to be the potential of having him *get* loose. We have to protect this ship."

Jessica stared into Cargo's eyes. He looked tired, as though he just couldn't wait for all of this to be over. At heart, Cargo loved the trade, the deals, seeing the wonders of the galaxy. Swashbuckling adventure? He could do it; he was more than competent with a weapon. But his heart wasn't in it.

This mission—what had turned into a thirty-year journey—was taking its toll on the man.

"I understand, Jessica. We do what we have to do for crew and ship. That's the way of it, right?"

Jessica nodded. It was. It always was.

"Cheeky still in medical, or is she in her quarters now?"

<Her quarters,> Sabrina replied. <Said if she had to spend another minute in the medbay she'd gouge her eyes out. I disapprove of gouging, so I encouraged her to move.>

"How considerate," Jessica said with a soft laugh.

"Don't take too long," Cargo said as he turned toward the cargo holds. "You still have to get armored up before our little confrontation."

"You bet," Jessica replied.

She walked down the passageway to the ladder that led up to the crew deck. She peeked into the galley, hoping to see Trevor, but he wasn't there.

<He left a little while ago, making sure that Ron's guys have everything set up.>

<What about you?> Jessica asked. <You ready to bust out of here at a moment's notice and lay down a beating if we have to take on Derrick's ship in space?>

<I don't like the idea of doing it alone,> Sabrina replied.

<You won't be alone. Finaeus, Misha, and Cheeky are all here.>

<I suppose. It would be good if Cheeky was on the bridge.>

Jessica nodded. She was sure Cheeky would feel the same way. <I'll ask her.>

<Thanks Jessica.>

Jessica knocked on the door to Cheeky's cabin, and a muffled 'come' answered her. She slid the door aside to reveal a darkened room with Cheeky laying on her bed, arm over her eyes.

"Head still hurt a lot?" Jessica asked quietly.

"Yuh, but better than before," Cheeky replied.

<The swelling in her brain has gone down, and the mednano are nearly done repairing damaged synapses. She'll be right as rain in a few hours,> Piya reported.

"And you, Piya?"

<I'm just fine. Nance's little magic trick didn't hit my Link port, so I came through OK, just worried about Cheeky.>

"I guess Nance didn't know as much about transference as she thought."

"Or she knew too much," Cheeky said softly.

"What do you mean?" Jessica asked.

"I don't know…she just felt weird. I did a transference with the AHAP. I know what it feels like to stretch my mind like that…the limitations…what Nance did felt entirely different. It's like she just walked right into my mind, pushed me aside, and made herself right at home."

<It was hard to see what she did,> Piya added. <Like Cheeky's mind was blurry, the ports to talk to her were closed while Nance was there. She just totally filled Cheeky's mind, did her thing, and then was gone.>

Jessica wondered how she'd feel in a situation like that. Having someone else take over your body would be unnerving no matter what, let alone while a massive antimatter bomb was right beside you.

"It's OK," Cheeky said. "She was in a rush...her first time. But she got the bomb disabled. We all lived, so no deliberate harm, no foul."

Jessica could tell that there was still something on Cheeky's mind, but decided not to push it. There would be plenty of time between the stars to talk further about what had happened.

"We don't anticipate anything going sideways, but do you think you could be on the bridge?" Jessica asked. "It would make Sabrina feel better."

<Pleeeeease,> Sabrina asked.

"You listening in, Sabs?" Cheeky asked.

<No, I just get an alert any time someone says my name. Since I knew Jessica was going to ask you about this, I popped in.>

Cheeky laughed, then groaned and held her head. "Oh, bad move." She took a slow breath and smiled weakly. "No need to get defensive, Sabs. I know you like to listen in on what's going on aboard. I'm not upset. Give me twenty and I'll be up there."

<Great! Thanks, Cheeky.>

"Just...just dim the lights and tone down the enthusiasm a bit, OK?"

<Of course, sorry,> Sabrina whispered in their minds.

"Sounds like everything will be well in hand," Jessica said. "Don't let Finaeus or Misha fly the ship while we're gone."

Cheeky gave a soft snort. "I may be messed up, but I'm not dead. Neither of those two are flying *Sabrina* while I still draw breath."

"That's the spirit," Jessica said, grinning as she rose.

"Hey Jess?" Cheeky asked as she departed.

"What is it, Cheeks?"

"When Derrick docks and you arrest his sorry ass, kick him in the balls for me, 'kay?"

Jessica chuckled. "Then he's getting it twice, because I already planned on it."

"Good deal," Cheeky replied.

THE DEAL WITH DERRICK
STELLAR DATE: 04.23.8940 (Adjusted Years)
LOCATION: Bay 295, Ellis Reach
REGION: Perry System, Stillwater Nebula, Perseus Arm

Derrick's ship, the *Cloud Singer*, eased into Bay 295 without any trouble at all. It wasn't a big ship, only half the length of *Sabrina*, but with more visible weaponry.

The bay's ramp rose up to the *Cloud Singer*'s starboard airlock, which cycled open to reveal Derrick in all his smarmy glory. Jessica eyed him from behind a stack of crates as he ambled down the ramp with a pair of women who wore medium armor and half-helmets trailing behind him.

For a moment, Jessica thought they were Macy and Jenn, but they were just two *other* butch, angry-looking women.

<Does he have a stable of them, or maybe a breeding program, or something?> Jessica asked.

<It's a big galaxy,> Iris replied. <I imagine that there's a stable of just about everything.>

<That's disturbing.>

Iris laughed. <I guess it is, I meant it metaphorically…but it's probably true in a non-metaphorical sense too.>

Ron waited at the bottom of the ramp with a pair of guards at his back, the same ones who had been with him when he'd taken Jessica and Trevor into custody.

In the intervening days, Jessica had gotten to know the two men, Andy and Karl. They were immeasurably happy not to have bombs in their heads anymore, and had gone on for some time about how they were looking forward to her time running the station.

She hadn't had the heart to tell them that once RHY had been led astray as to the existence of *Sabrina* she would be leaving.

Although, she had to put someone in charge of the place. Though she trusted Ron enough to meet with Derrick—especially when Jessica held a high-powered rifle that was currently aimed at Derrick's head—she didn't trust him to make a good, long-term, ruler for The Reach, and the Perry System in general.

He was a doer, but lacked the cunning to keep a place like this from falling to the next mini-dictator wannabe.

Jessica watched Ron stretch out his hand to take Derrick's. "Took you long enough," Ron said. "You were supposed to be here before them. Good thing The Perry had me around to get them locked down and under control."

"So you got them? They're secure? And their ship?" Derrick asked, barely able to hide how eager he was.

"Yeah, the purple girl and her hulk came off the ship and I nabbed 'em. Then we spent a bit negotiating with the ship and when the time came to do the handoff, we managed to get them with a fast-acting nerve gas and stormed the thing."

"That's it? That easy?" Derrick asked, a look of skepticism crossing his face."

"Easy? It took three days and I lost two men doing it. Not what I call easy."

Derrick nodded, though he looked as though he still didn't quite believe Ron.

"Show me."

"No can do." Ron shook his head. "First you're going to meet The Perry to talk terms."

Derrick sneered down at Ron. "I laid out my terms already. It was in the bounty."

Ron didn't bite, and instead shrugged nonchalantly. "Well, we have the ship and *Retyna Girl*, who is worth a hell of a lot more than you're offering. So, I guess we'll see if you can up the payment."

Derrick sputtered, and Jessica enjoyed watching him struggle to find his next words. "Fine. Take me to The Perry. How's Simon doing these days, anyway? Still disgusting?"

"Oh," Ron replied casually. "Simon's not The Perry anymore. We're under new management."

"Then who is it?" Derrick asked.

"Me," Jessica said as she stepped out around the crates with her rifle shouldered and a face-splitting grin plastered on. "I bet this isn't how you expected to meet next, is it?"

"You?" Derrick sputtered and took a step back. "Damnit!"

"Can't kill me, right?" Jessica asked. "I'm worth a fortune because of my pretty purple skin. Thing is, the previous Perry told RHY about me, so they're coming to collect soon—so no finder's fee there for you."

Derrick sighed and took another step back, his new girls moving in front of him.

"Not going to help much," Cargo said as he emerged from behind one of the docking cradle's struts. "Holes in your back work just as well as ones in the front."

Trevor emerged a moment later from the other side and Derrick looked around with growing alarm as a dozen more armored figures stepped into view around the bay.

"I see you've made a name for yourself here, Retyna Girl," Derrick sneered. "But don't think for a second that I'm just going to surrender. My SC Batts are charged, and my weapons are hot. Mess with me and I tear this station apart from the inside."

Jessica nodded slowly. "Yeah, assholes like you like to do things like that. Cool thing about the old Perry. He was a paranoid sumbitch. This bay here? It's for folks who were worth the trouble, but not trustworthy. Get my drift?"

Derrick's face fell and his lips finally lost their sneer. "There's a spiker in here."

"Yup, focused right on your ship. A six-emitter one too, I'm told that's enough to crush your vessel down into a nice little ball of trash, seeing's how your shields are down and your reactors are offline."

"You won't do it. I have antimatter aboard."

"No, you don't. You took the comms hookup when the station power umbilical connected. My AI, Iris, has already hacked your systems, and found that your bottle is empty—not that we were worried. You didn't do a single AP burn coming in system, and we knew you'd be in a rush. Must have used it all up trying to beat us here."

"Fuck."

"Ladies," Jessica addressed Derrick's two guards. "I don't know what this dickhead means to you, but I sure hope you don't think he's worth dying for."

One of the women looked at the other, and then slowly set her weapon on the deck. The second woman followed a moment later.

"Helmets too," Jessica added. "Then get on the ground."

The women did as Jessica instructed, but Derrick still stood, a sulk on his face. "You too asshat," Jessica said, pointing at the deck with the barrel of her gun.

Derrick hesitated, and she fired a shot over his shoulder, tearing the epaulette off his fancy jacket. The bullet ricocheted off the ramp and shards of the projectile shot into the airlock behind Derrick.

Jessica took a step closer, her rifle's barrel aimed right between the sleazebag's eyes. "Good people tell me that killing you would be wrong, Derrick. But to be honest, I think they'd still let me get away with it."

"I sure would," Trevor rumbled. "You've been very unkind to my wife."

"Wife?" Derrick asked.

Trevor nodded as he stepped closer to the man, looming over him.

"OK!" Derrick shouted and got down on the deck.

"Hands behind your head, legs spread," Trevor hollered before putting an armored knee into Derrick's back.

Jessica knelt by his head. "I bet you're really regretting taking that call from Macy and Jenn all those years ago, aren't you?"

Derrick nodded, his cheek pressed against the deck. "I really am…."

Ron's guards moved in and helped secure the two women and Derrick, while Cargo and Trevor walked up the ramp to inspect Derrick's ship.

"Good work, Ron," Jessica said, clasping the man's shoulder. "Couldn't have done this without you."

Ron smiled, a genuine smile from a man who had been very lacking in positive reinforcement over the years.

"Thanks, Perina. Was my pleasure."

BETTER THAN YOU FOUND IT
STELLAR DATE: 05.15.8940 (Adjusted Years)
LOCATION: The Perina's offices, Ellis Reach
REGION: Perry System, Stillwater Nebula, Perseus Arm

<Oria, have we heard back from Viceroy Station yet? I called in for their stationmaster to come over here an hour ago,> Jessica asked the Ellis Reach's new station AI.

<I just got a response, Jessica. He's going to leave in a few hours. Should take him just under two days to get here.>

<Thanks Oria, he'll be the last one,> Jessica replied with a tired sigh.

<Do you think he'll be any trouble?> Oria asked.

<No, I think he'll be the easiest of the bunch, that's why I left him for last.>

The past three weeks had gone by in a strange combination of excruciating slowness, and a whirlwind of activity. The crew of *Sabrina* had wrought so many changes on Ellis Reach that the station—which it could now be called without any possibility of incarceration—was barely recognizable.

Ron was now the head of a properly organized police force, and was doing his best to live up to the trust Jessica had placed in him. He still reverted to force and coercion when he didn't know what else to do, but the pair of AIs Jessica had established in the police administration were helping him learn the value of a measured response.

Placing Ron in a position of authority was one Jessica and the team had debated for some time. In the end, they all had to admit they were still in a system filled with an overabundance of less-savory types. Extortion had been the name of the game here for centuries, and Ron knew many of the players, and what skeletons were in their closets.

Like Brooke. It turned out she had extorted so much money during her 'inspections' that she was one of the wealthiest people in the system. She had also tried to charter a ship to get off The Reach the day Derrick had been arrested.

Ron had gleefully picked her up and put her in the slammer. It seemed that the two had never been fans of one another.

The hardest thing—at least thus far—had been finding a judge to form the backbone of a fair court system. The Reach had never been a place that engendered trust, and there weren't many people considered to be fair and impartial.

It was Cheeky who brought the solution—the bartender named Bill. It turned out Bill had always given everyone an ear, and never told any tales. He had informally arbitrated dozens of disputes on the station over the years, and people often came to him for advice.

He had been nervous about the idea, but he was now the system's one and only Judge. Hopefully, as they established reasonable laws, he would be able to help keep things on an even footing.

<*I bet when you got all pissed off about having to clean those tanks, you didn't expect deposing The Perry to turn into this, did you?*> Iris asked.

<*I wasn't thinking much about anything,*> Jessica replied. <*I was just…I was depressed, honestly. I'd had so much purpose with the kids, raising them, caring for them, teaching them. Then it was like it had never happened. We were just back on the ship, hopping from system to system.*>

<*You went a little stir-crazy.*>

Jessica laughed. <*A little?*>

<*Well, Trevor and I kept you in line…mostly.*>

Jessica looked around the large, oak-paneled offices, and through the windows at the simulation of Lake Athabasca, and its low waves lapping at edge of the sand dune desert on its southern shores.

<*You're right about one thing, though. I sure didn't expect this. But who knows how long RHY could take to show—if they even show at all. I think that we need to set a departure date and work toward that.*>

Iris nodded in agreement within Jessica's mind. <*I think you're right. We still have a long road ahead. We can't linger here forever.*>

<*Which means I need to get cracking on finding a new Perry or Perina to take over after me,*> Jessica replied.

She summoned the list of candidates she'd been going over. The Perry System wasn't densely populated. A dozen major stations, the largest of which was Ellis Reach with its ten-thousand occupants. All told, the system barely had one hundred-fifty thousand inhabitants.

<*Have you considered an AI?*> Iris asked.

Jessica bit her lip. She had, but she didn't think it would work—at least not yet. One of the first things the AIs from *Sabrina* had insisted on was the liberation and enlightenment of the AIs on The Reach—of which there were seven. Sabrina had created an expanse, and helped the AIs learn and grow.

The Reach's AIs had been blown away by how limited they'd been, and how they hadn't even known. In a matter of days, they had taken up tasks which had helped the people immeasurably, and earned their trust.

Oria was especially good at station management, and had identified and repaired hundreds of failures while working with the maintenance teams to turn The Reach into a top-notch facility.

Jessica had considered offering Oria the job of Perry, but the AI really seemed to revel in managing the systems, and the comings and goings of people insofar as organizing timelines was concerned, but she had no desire to deal with the actual interpersonal conflicts.

<I've looked them over,> Jessica said after she'd considered her words carefully. <But I don't think they're ready—the AIs, or the people here.>

<You're probably right,> Iris said after a moment. <Whoever takes this on is going to have a rough time. The AIs are still coming to grips with what it is that they are—dealing with that **and** managing a whole station full of you crazy organics would be too much. But you're going to have to find someone soon. It'll take time to transition them into the role.>

<What do you think about…an election?> Jessica proposed.

Iris snorted. <Do you think these people are ready for self-governance? They have virtually no experience in it.>

<Maybe someone will step forward, someone with the gumption to get the job done. Getting elected by their peers would help them get the confidence boost, versus me just appointing someone.>

<Look at you, all governoring,> Iris said with a smile. <Tanis would be proud.>

Jessica laughed aloud. <Just feels good to finally leave a place in better shape than we found it in.>

<Perina!> Oria interrupted her thoughts. *<I have five ships on scan, approaching the station.>*

Jessica wondered what had facilitated the alarm. The Perry Strait wasn't the busiest place in the galaxy, but there were always a few ships on inbound vectors.

<Why the alarm?> she asked.

<They didn't fly in through the system…they just…appeared.>

"Shit!" Jessica swore. *<How far?>*

<They're one AU from Seaway, and not moving too fast. If they maintain their current vector, they'll be here in…oh, nope, they're accelerating. I give them four hours.>

<OK, everyone,> Jessica called into *Sabrina*'s shipnet. *<Our guests have arrived. They jumped in. We have four hours until they arrive.>*

<Say what?> Cheeky exclaimed. *<Four hours? How are we going to be ready in four hours?>*

<You better get back down to medical,> Jessica advised. *<You're about to become Retyna Girl.>*

JUMP GATE
STELLAR DATE: 05.15.8940 (Adjusted Years)
LOCATION: The Perina's offices, Ellis Reach
REGION: Perry System, Stillwater Nebula, Perseus Arm

"Hot damn, you look good purple!" Jessica said when Cheeky walked into her office.

Cheeky spun and gave a short bow. "Discount Retyna Girl at your service."

Jessica rose to look Cheeky over, nodding with satisfaction. Her skin was purple—though a slightly different shade—as was her hair. She wore tall heels to approach Jessica's height, and the purple skinsuit made her look curvier than she was naturally.

The best part was the glow. Finaeus had nailed it, specifically by *not* nailing it. Rather than the variations of Jessica's bioluminescent glow, Cheeky's was well-nigh neon. It was both very purple, and very much the wrong purple.

"Finaeus did a great job," Cheeky said with a wink. "Somehow he made me look as much like a sex-bot as you without having to pull out half my ribs."

"Hey," Jessica said, patting her abdomen. "I'm only missing two ribs, not half. Those ones are extra, anyway.

How are you managing with all that pesky clothing touching you?"

Cheeky laughed. "Finaeus did something to my sense of touch when he made my skin glow. I can barely feel anything," Cheeky said as she pushed on her cheeks. "It's really weird."

"Yes, well, stop touching yourself like that," Addie said, shaking her head as she came into the room behind Cheeky. Today, however, Autonomous Human Assimilation Personage wasn't Addie. She was the new Perina.

The AHAP appeared to be a tall, white-haired woman with a severe expression, and piercing eyes. She exuded power and control in her dark suit.

Although Jessica had worked to ensure that no images of herself had leaked out after she'd seized control, she knew that it would be impossible to hide the fact that a Perina was now in control of the system. Hence the AHAP masquerading as the woman in charge.

"How do you like your office?" Jessica asked.

The new Perina walked around the space, examining it with a critical eye. "I suppose it will do. The décor is not quite to my taste, but we're on a short timeline here." The Perina stopped and ran a finger along a counter. "Needs to be dusted as well."

"Finaeus, cut it out." Cheeky laughed.

"Oh! So you opted not to let Addie run with this herself?" Jessica asked with a raised eyebrow.

Finaeus-Perina nodded. "Addie probably could have—stars, she did *you* for several days back at Serenity. But I've been getting bored. Plus, I wanted to try this out, see how it works. It's very convincing. I actually feel like I'm *in* this body. I've got a nice set of knockers too."

"Finaeus. Stop that, it's unseemly," Cheeky admonished.

Finaeus-Perina snorted. "I adore you Cheeky, but you live in a glass house when it comes to *unseemly*."

Jessica laughed, and Cheeky blushed…or, rather, her neon purple glow took on a slight pink hue.

"Sorry that you have to hide so much, Finaeus," Jessica replied as she leaned against the desk. "If you weren't so damn famous…."

"Or infamous." Finaeus-Perry chuckled. "But thank you, I appreciate the sentiment. It's nice to go for a stroll and not have to worry about people spotting me. There's only so much I can do in the small lab I've carved out on *Sabrina*. Especially with how much time we spend in the dark layer. There are a lot of experiments that are far too risky to run in there."

"I really don't like that you run experiments aboard the ship at all," Cheeky said with a long-suffering sigh.

"Cheeky, my beautiful blueberry, I've survived for over five thousand years running experiments of nearly every sort you can imagine. I've never—well, very, very rarely have I blown up the ship I was on."

"So much confidence has just *not* been established," Cheeky replied.

<The RHY ships are within a light-second now,> Oria advised. <I suppose you're in charge now, Finaeus?>

"My dear Oria, I'm always in charge," Finaeus said as he-she sat at the desk and spread his-her hands on the mahogany surface. "Hail them."

<Of course, grand Perina.>

"Wait!" Jessica called out. "Finaeus, we need guards. You're not just going to have fake Retyna Girl in here on her own."

Finaeus frowned. "I suppose not, though I bet I could take her. Especially with Addie's body. Jessica, go fetch Andy and Karl. They're in on all this, right?"

"Stars," Jessica muttered. "Yes. I'll be in the hall watching over the Link."

Jessica walked out of the room and beckoned Andy and Karl. "You're up, guys. Be gentle with Cheeky, she's not as tough as she likes to think she is."

"You got it, Perina," Andy said with a nod. "Kid gloves, that's us."

Jessica leaned back against the wall and brought up the room in her mind, watching and praying that Finaeus wouldn't do anything stupid.

It wasn't that she didn't trust the man, he just had a habit of not taking things seriously enough.

<Kinda like **you** at the beginning of this little adventure?> Iris asked.

Jessica drew in a deep breath and let it out slowly before responding. <I suppose, yeah. I was a bit blasé, wasn't I?>

<Reckless would be more like it. You're lucky Trevor and I are so patient. We both agreed to let you get whatever it was out of your system.>

<I'm starting to feel ganged up on. You talk about me behind my back?> Jessica asked with a quiet laugh. She knew they did. The pair had become close friends over the years, even more so during their time in The Dream.

<Frequently, yeah,> Iris said with a smirk. <Seriously, though, I'm glad that being the Perina has helped you get your head back on straight, even though I would never have guessed that head-straightening would be a possible outcome.>

Jessica laughed aloud. <You know me, give me a star system to run and I perk right up.>

<I'll keep that in mind.>

Via her monitoring on the Link, Jessica saw that Oria had connected Finaeus and the RHY representative. She set aside her thoughts of how being the Perina had brought her out of her empty-nester's slump. Maybe she had needed something important to take care of....

In the room next door, Finaeus-Perina said, "Welcome to the Perry System," as a holographic figure appeared before his desk.

The RHY representative was a man, and bore a striking familial resemblance to Phoebe, the marketing executive they had met in the Naga System.

<My money is on cousin,> Iris commented. <Phoebe said her uncle runs RHY, and I can't imagine him coming out here to grab you.>

<If they have jump gates it's not a long trip, though,> Jessica replied.

<Here, no. Back, yes.>

<Unless they plan to make a gate here,> Jessica said, worried that RHY would do just that. No one in the Perry System would benefit from that happening—though it would change the face of trade in the Stillwater Nebula.

<If we couldn't build one at Star City because of its proximity to the nebula, I don't see how they could build one *in* it,> Iris replied

While Jessica and Iris had discussed gates and the man's relationship to Phoebe, he had responded.

"Greetings Perina. My name is Rath, vice-president of RHY's R-Bio Division. We received word that you have found the person who was used as the model for Retyna Girl in the Naga System several years ago."

"I have, yes," Finaeus-Perina nodded slowly, eyes narrowed. "I knew that she was of some value to you, but for you to send in five ships…and via jump gate if I don't miss my guess…."

Rath nodded slowly. "I was wondering if you knew about jump gates out here. To be honest, I wasn't even aware that there were settled systems this deep in Stillwater. It's very curious."

"Word tends to get around," Finaeus-Perina replied. "About jump gates, that is. Even for those of us just trying to scratch out a living out here."

"So, you said that you have the woman named Jessica, who was injected with our product for her shoot as Retyna Girl. You sent back some very convincing video of her, but now I'd like to see her myself."

Finaeus-Perina smiled coolly. "I'd like to know what you're willing to offer in trade for her. From what I saw in the news feeds, you took a very large hit when you lost the Retyna product line."

Rath snorted. "More than your system pulls in over ten years, I imagine. Now show her to me or we leave now."

Finaeus-Perina sighed, and waved her hand to indicate Cheeky, who was bracketed by Andy and Karl—who held her arms. Cheeky, for her part, looked exceptionally morose—her hair was disheveled and she slouched in the grip of the guards.

"Show me her face," Rath said without an ounce of compassion in his voice. Andy reached over and pushed Cheeky's purple hair aside, then shoved her head back—not too roughly, but enough for Rath to believe she was a prisoner.

"What's with her skin? Is it degrading? She doesn't look right at all," Rath said, turning to someone next to him who wasn't being projected.

A moment later he pulled another person into view, and Jessica almost laughed to see Phoebe. The woman was alive, which Jessica had hoped wouldn't be the case after the explosion on Hermes station, but her joy was derived from how mortified Phoebe appeared to be.

"But…we saw vid…she was here! You have to believe me Rath, the person in the vid was her! I don't know who this girl is, but we have to find Jessica! She has the microbes; I know—"

"I assure you," Finaeus-Perina interrupted, "this is the same girl. I have Retyna Girl. If you'd just dock and come see her, I'm certain that you'll realize she's the genuine article."

Rath pushed Phoebe back out of view. "That's it Phoebe. That's it. Third strike and you're out. You've had me flying all over the OFA chasing Retyna Girl sightings. And this time we just had to jump into the ass crack of nowhere. You're finished."

They could hear Phoebe wail off camera, and Finaeus-Perina spoke up again. "Please, come to the station, see her for yourself. Take samples."

"Do you take me for a fool?" Rath replied. "So I can become your next hostage? I don't think so...though I have half a mind to send you Phoebe. Maybe she could do some promotional work for your...whatever it is you do out here. Fuck knows she's finished at RHY, even if dad does owe your father a favor or two still." He said the last facing away at where Jessica presumed Phoebe stood.

"I'm open to that, we could use her to—" Finaeus-Perina said, but the connection closed and Rath was gone.

Jessica opened the door and walked back into the office. "I can barely believe that just happened. Did that just happen?"

Cheeky tapped Andy on the arm and winked at him. "You can let me go now."

Andy coughed and stepped back. "Sorry I was a bit rough there."

"Rough?" Cheeky laughed before giving Andy a slow wink. "Seriously? That's not even close to rough."

"Uhh…I feel very uncomfortable right now," Andy said and turned to Jessica. "Can we go?"

"Yeah, good work, guys. Take the rest of the day off," Jessica said and patted them each on the shoulder as they walked past.

<The RHY ships are doing something,> Oria said, a nervous tone to her voice.

Jessica put the view of the five ships on the room's holoprojector. The ships had all ceased decelerating, and one of them was deploying a series of objects.

<Is it a weapon?> Oria asked.

"No," Finaeus-Perina replied, his-her eyes widening. "It's a jump gate."

Over the next hour, the RHY ships constructed the jump gate, their vector bringing them closer and closer to Seaway. As they watched, the rest of *Sabrina*'s crew had joined them in the Perina's office, watching as the RHY ships constructed a doorway home.

"Shit," Finaeus muttered. "They're going to let it fall into the planet when they're done."

<It'll take another two hours before it hits the cloud tops,> Oria said.

<I could get there in time if we leave in the next thirty minutes,> Sabrina chimed in. <We could jump to New Canaan! Get this mission over with.>

The crew began talking excitedly about packing up and going, Nance almost jumping for joy, but while they spoke, an uncomfortable feeling settled in the pit of Jessica's stomach.

"I don't know if I can go," she said softly.

Trevor was beside her, and seemed to be the only one to hear her utterance. "What do you mean, you can't go," he asked.

"We're not done here," Jessica replied. "This system is far from stable. If we go now, some new despot is going to rise up in no time and take over again. You saw how happy these people were to have a real leader who cares about them," Jessica said. "I owe it to them not to show how good it can be, and then snatch it away."

"You can't be serious," Cargo asked, having overheard Jessica. "You've wanted to get back to New Canaan for years. Now we have the express road home and you don't want to take it?"

"I *want* to," Jessica said. "But I don't think I *can*. Besides, it's a big risk. If we rush out there with *Sabrina*, who's to say that we can use the gate in time. They'll see the ship for sure. Then the jig will be up too."

"Yeah," Nance said, "But so what? If we leave through a jump gate, it's not like they can follow. We'll be out. Home free."

"They'll see us approaching," Finaeus cautioned. "If they spot *Sabrina*, they're not just going to let us come on over and use the gate."

<We can take them,> Sabrina said. <They're not so tough. Stars, I could ram them if I had to.>

"And then what?" Jessica asked. "Then all of Perseus knows we were here. What if we can't get the gate to work for us before it hits the planet? It's not like we can just walk up to it and dial home, right Finaeus?"

Finaeus-Perina nodded slowly. "It's true. They'll use different control interfaces. It might take some time before I could make it work for us."

"Don't you want to try, Jessica?" Cheeky asked.

"I *do*," Jessica said. "I have a lot of friends from the *Intrepid* that I haven't seen in years. I miss Tanis terribly, but we have a real chance to do some good here in Perseus. We can help these people establish a good government and prosper. We've already liberated the AIs here on The Reach, and we can do the rest of the stations in the system too. They can be a beacon for other AIs on the Stillwater passage."

She looked at each of the crewmembers, one after another, imploring them to understand.

"Look, if you all want to go, I understand. Tanis and Sera need Finaeus. Getting him back there as soon as possible is a good thing. But I have to stay."

"Well if you stay, I stay," Trevor said. "I'm in all this for you, after all."

"This is asinine!" Cheeky exclaimed. "We're not splitting up. No way, no how."

<*I could dispatch a pair of tugs,*> Oria suggested. <*They could try to grab the jump gate before it gets too close to the planet.*>

"OK, do that," Jessica replied. "But even if we do secure it, I'm not leaving till we have a new government in place. For once, we're going to clean a system up, rather than fuck it up."

There were slow nods from the rest of the crew, though Nance appeared to be exceedingly reticent in her gesture of acquiescence.

<*Tugs are outbound,*> Oria announced. <*We had two in the vicinity. They should reach the gate in seventy minutes.*>

The crew didn't speak much as they watched the minutes tick by. Jessica felt guilty that she'd strong-armed them into staying, but Iris reassured her that it had been the right call.

<*Staying to help these people out aside, revealing* Sabrina *would have been a bad move. If RHY spotted the ship, it would*

have undone everything we've worked toward for the past three years. It's the right thing to do,> Iris said.

Forty-five minutes later, the ring came to life and the first of the RHY ships disappeared through it, followed by another two a minute later, but the last pair hung back.

<They've sent a message to the tugs,> Oria said. <Told them to turn back, or be fired on. What should I do?>

Jessica blew out a long breath. "Tell them to turn back."

<Sending,> Oria replied.

No one spoke as the holoprojection showed the tugs breaking and changing vector to return to The Reach. The final two RHY ships stayed with the ring until it was only five thousand kilometers from Seaway's roiling cloud tops. Then they too passed through the ring minutes before it fell into the planet.

"It'll explode in about seven minutes," Finaeus-Perina said. "I wonder if they managed to use the planet's gravity to help counteract the nebula, or if they just ended up on the far side of the galaxy...."

"Shit," Cheeky muttered. "I hadn't thought of that. Do you think they knew what the nebula would do to their trajectory?"

"I rather hope they didn't," Nance replied crossly.

"Doesn't matter," Cargo replied with a long sigh. "It's gone now. I'm going to go catch some sack."

Cheeky looked around at the team and gave a wan smile. "Well, on the bright side, not a single person died on this excursion."

"Thank the stars for small miracles," Jessica replied.

ON THE ROAD AGAIN
STELLAR DATE: 01.12.8941 (Adjusted Years)
LOCATION: *Sabrina*
REGION: Departing Perry System, Stillwater Nebula, Perseus Arm

Eight months later...

Jessica sat in *Sabrina*'s rear observation lounge, watching the star at the center of the Perry System dwindle to just another point of light; it's feeble glow pushing against the dense clouds surrounding it, little more than just another mote, swimming in the glow of the Stillwater Nebula.

<*I'm proud of what we did there,*> she said to Iris. <*We made a real thing, maybe it can even be a lasting thing.*>

<*It doesn't have to last forever for it to be worth doing,*> Iris replied. <*Even a day of joy is better than none at all.*>

<*Is that an old proverb or something?*> Jessica asked.

<*Yes, an AI proverb.*>

<*Huh?*> Jessica said. <*I didn't know AIs had proverbs.*>

<*A few,*> Iris said with a laugh. <*A few million.*>

<*I imagine we humans must too,*> Jessica replied then fell silent once more.

Iris spoke up after a moment. <*They're going to do well. They elected a government, they believe in their leadership — mostly.*>

<Mostly,> Jessica snorted. <Stars, I hope they pull it off. Can you believe they elected Karl?>

<Who knew that he used to run a whole planet.... That's what he gets for trying to escape his past.>

Jessica nodded, that thought leading her to another. <Do you think they'll stop giving me the cold shoulder?>

<Cargo and Nance?> Iris asked. <Eventually, yeah. Finaeus knew it wasn't possible, but Nance...she really wanted to go home. Misha doesn't really care—so long as he has a full larder, he's happy.>

<And Cheeky...> Jessica said with a sigh. <She acts normal, but I wonder if she resents me now.>

<You're Cheeky's best friend, Jessica. You know she has your back. She's not duplicitous. The Cheeky you see is the Cheeky you get.>

The door slid open and Trevor entered. "About to hit the dark layer. You want to come to the bridge?"

Jessica shook her head. "Not this time, I want to watch it till it's gone."

Trevor sat beside Jessica and wrapped an arm around her. "I liked it there. Pretty good place, considering our rocky start."

"Pretty good place," Jessica agreed. "It's surprising how—out here at the far end of nowhere—we're meeting so many good people...but we're in Orion space. They're supposed to be the enemy."

"You know how it is, Jess, these people don't even know that there's a war brewing. They're decades from the front lines. Stars, places like the Perry System have probably never even seen an OFA representative come through."

"And let's hope they never do," Jessica replied.

"I wonder what Derrick will think when he comes to?" Trevor asked.

Jessica chuckled softly. "Well, that light-hugger was making a fifty-year run. After his nap, nothing he does will matter anymore."

"What are the chances the captain of that freighter is going to dump Derrick in a prison when he gets out there?"

Jessica shrugged. "Feels fifty-fifty to me, but I guess we'll never know."

"Guess not," Trevor replied.

The pair sat and watched the view out of the window on the back of the ship until *Sabrina* transitioned and there was nothing but darkness beyond the running lights above the engines.

"You game for a round of Snark?" Trevor asked after a few minutes of silence. "I picked up a new variant back on The Reach."

Jessica looked up into his large, expressive eyes and nodded. "Sure. Might as well spank you again."

"Well, hey, if spanking is what you want to get up to..."

"Cards first," Jessica replied with a wink. "Then we'll see how things go."

THE END

* * * * *

Though they've made it past the Stillwater Nebula, Jessica and the crew have a long way to go. They're still thousands of light years deep in Orion space and over a decade from home.

Find out how they make it back to New Canaan in ***The Final Stroll on Perseus's Arm***.

THE BOOKS OF AEON 14

Keep up to date with what is releasing in Aeon 14 with the free Aeon 14 Reading Guide.

Origins of Destiny (The Age of Terra)
- Prequel: Storming the Norse Wind
- Book 1: Shore Leave (in Galactic Genesis until Sept 2018)
- Book 2: Operative (Summer 2018)
- Book 3: Blackest Night (Summer 2018)

The Intrepid Saga (The Age of Terra)
- Book 1: Outsystem
- Book 2: A Path in the Darkness
- Book 3: Building Victoria

- The Intrepid Saga Omnibus – *Also contains Destiny Lost, book 1 of the Orion War series*

- Destiny Rising – *Special Author's Extended Edition comprised of both Outsystem and A Path in the Darkness with over 100 pages of new content.*

The Orion War
- Book 1: Destiny Lost
- Book 2: New Canaan
- Book 3: Orion Rising
- Book 4: The Scipio Alliance
- Book 5: Attack on Thebes
- Book 6: War on a Thousand Fronts
- Book 7: Fallen Empire (2018)
- Book 8: Airtha Ascendancy (2018)
- Book 9: The Orion Front (2018)
- Book 10: Starfire (2019)
- Book 11: Race Across Time (2019)
- Book 12: Return to Sol (2019)

Tales of the Orion War
- Book 1: Set the Galaxy on Fire
- Book 2: Ignite the Stars
- Book 3: Burn the Galaxy to Ash (2018)

Perilous Alliance (Age of the Orion War – w/Chris J. Pike)
- Book 1: Close Proximity
- Book 2: Strike Vector
- Book 3: Collision Course
- Book 4: Impact Imminent
- Book 5: Critical Inertia (Sept 2018)

Rika's Marauders (Age of the Orion War)
- Prequel: Rika Mechanized
- Book 1: Rika Outcast
- Book 2: Rika Redeemed
- Book 3: Rika Triumphant
- Book 4: Rika Commander
- Book 5: Rika Infiltrator
- Book 6: Rika Unleashed (2018)
- Book 7: Rika Conqueror (2019)

Perseus Gate (Age of the Orion War)
Season 1: Orion Space
- Episode 1: The Gate at the Grey Wolf Star
- Episode 2: The World at the Edge of Space
- Episode 3: The Dance on the Moons of Serenity
- Episode 4: The Last Bastion of Star City
- Episode 5: The Toll Road Between the Stars
- Episode 6: The Final Stroll on Perseus's Arm
- Eps 1-3 Omnibus: The Trail Through the Stars
- Eps 4-6 Omnibus: The Path Amongst the Clouds

Season 2: Inner Stars
- Episode 1: A Meeting of Bodies and Minds
- Episode 3: A Deception and a Promise Kept
- Episode 3: A Surreptitious Rescue of Friends and Foes (2018)

PERSEUS GATE: SEASON 1 – THE TOLL ROAD BETWEEN THE STARS

- Episode 4: A Trial and the Tribulations (2018)
- Episode 5: A Deal and a True Story Told (2018)
- Episode 6: A New Empire and An Old Ally (2018)

Season 3: AI Empire
- Episode 1: Restitution and Recompense (2019)
- Five more episodes following...

The Warlord (Before the Age of the Orion War)
- Book 1: The Woman Without a World
- Book 2: The Woman Who Seized an Empire
- Book 3: The Woman Who Lost Everything

The Sentience Wars: Origins (Age of the Sentience Wars – w/James S. Aaron)
- Book 1: Lyssa's Dream
- Book 2: Lyssa's Run
- Book 3: Lyssa's Flight
- Book 4: Lyssa's Call
- Book 5: Lyssa's Flame

Legends of the Sentience Wars (Age of the Sentience Wars – w/James S. Aaron)
- Volume 1: The Proteus Bridge (August 2018)

Enfield Genesis (Age of the Sentience Wars – w/Lisa Richman)
- Book 1: Alpha Centauri
- Book 2: Proxima Centauri (2018)

Hand's Assassin (Age of the Orion War – w/T.G. Ayer)
- Book 1: Death Dealer
- Book 2: Death Mark (August 2018)

Machete System Bounty Hunter (Age of the Orion War – w/Zen DiPietro)
- Book 1: Hired Gun
- Book 2: Gunning for Trouble
- Book 3: With Guns Blazing

Vexa Legacy (Age of the FTL Wars – w/Andrew Gates)
- Book 1: Seas of the Red Star

Building New Canaan (Age of the Orion War – w/J.J. Green)
- Book 1: Carthage
- Book 2: Tyre (2018)

Fennington Station Murder Mysteries (Age of the Orion War)
- Book 1: Whole Latte Death (w/Chris J. Pike)
- Book 2: Cocoa Crush (w/Chris J. Pike)

The Empire (Age of the Orion War)
- The Empress and the Ambassador (2018)
- Consort of the Scorpion Empress (2018)
- By the Empress's Command (2018)

The Sol Dissolution (The Age of Terra)
- Book 1: Venusian Uprising (2018)
- Book 2: Scattered Disk (2018)
- Book 3: Jovian Offensive (2019)
- Book 4: Fall of Terra (2019)

ABOUT THE AUTHOR

Michael Cooper likes to think of himself as a jack-of-all-trades (and hopes to become master of a few). When not writing, he can be found writing software, working in his shop at his latest carpentry project, or likely reading a book.

He shares his home with a precocious young girl, his wonderful wife (who also writes), two cats, a never-ending list of things he would like to build, and ideas...

Find out what's coming next at www.aeon14.com

Made in the USA
San Bernardino, CA
31 August 2018